There was another flash and explosion, even brighter, louder, and closer than the first one. Suddenly stuff was flying all over us. Dirt. Clumps of mud. Sticks, grass, rocks, pieces of tree bark.

It was like we were caught in the middle of a tornado. But this stuff wasn't swirling around, the way I'd imagine a tornado must throw stuff around. It was just flying every which way.

This was no earthquake or volcano or hurricane. No, nature couldn't produce this kind of violence. Somebody was *shooting* at us.

Also by Dan Gutman

The Get Rich Quick Club

Johnny Hangtime

My Weird School:

Miss Daisy Is Crazy!

Mr. Klutz Is Nuts!

Mrs. Roopy Is Loopy!

Ms. Hannah Is Bananas!

Miss Small Is off the Wall!

Mr. Hynde Is Out of His Mind!

Mrs. Cooney Is Loony!

Ms. LaGrange Is Strange!

Miss Lazar Is Bizarre!

Mr. Docker Is Off His Rocker!

Mrs. Kormel Is Not Normal!

Ms. Todd Is Odd!

Mrs. Patty Is Batty!

Miss Holly Is Too Jolly!

Baseball Card Adventures:

Honus & Me

Jackie & Me

Babe & Me

Shoeless Joe & Me

Mickey & Me

Satch & Me

Abner & Me

A Baseball Card Adventure

Dan Gutman

HarperTrophy®
An Imprint of HarperCollins*Publishers*

Abner & Me

www.harpercollinschildrens.com

Library of Congress Cataloging-in-Publication Data
Gutman, Dan.
Abner & me : a baseball card adventure / Dan Gutman.—1st ed.
p. cm.
Summary: With his ability to travel through time using baseball cards and photographs, thirteen-year-old Joe and his mother go back to 1863 to ask Abner Doubleday whether he invented baseball, but instead find themselves in the middle of the Battle of Gettysburg.
ISBN-10: 0-06-053445-1 — ISBN-13: 978-0-06-053445-5
Doubleday, Abner, 1819–1893—Juvenile fiction. [1. Doubleday, Abner, 1819–1893—Fiction. 2. Time travel—Fiction. 3. Baseball—Fiction. 4. Gettysburg, Battle of, Gettysburg, Pa., 1863—Fiction. 5. Mothers and sons—Fiction. 6. Baseball cards—Fiction. 7. United States—History—Civil War, 1861–1865—Fiction.] I. Title: Abner and me. II. Title.
PZ7.G9846Ab 2005 2004006315
[Fic]—dc22 CIP
AC

❖

First Harper Trophy edition, 2007

Dedicated to Stephen Fraser,
Elise Howard, and all the folks
at HarperCollins Children's Books

Acknowledgments

Thanks to David Kelly of the Library of Congress, Ryan Chamberlain of the Society for American Baseball Research, Bill Burdick at the National Baseball Hall of Fame, Barry "Magnet" Aguado of the New York Mutuals, and Nina Wallace.

Author's Note

This book contains more violent scenes than my previous books. It may not be suitable for younger readers.

1

Anti-Social Studies

"HEY, WHAT'S UP WITH YOU, STOSHACK?"

Kenny Cohen was whispering from the seat behind mine. It was the middle of social studies and Mrs. Van Hook was giving a boring lecture about the Civil War. Something about the Missouri Compromise. Learning about battles and stuff was pretty cool, but all that junk about what led up to the war didn't interest me much.

"What do you mean, what's up with me?" I asked, leaning back in my chair so Mrs. Van Hook wouldn't catch me whispering to Kenny.

"People are talking about you, man."

"Oh yeah?" I asked Kenny. "And what are these people saying?"

"They're saying you're a freak. They're saying you got magic powers or something."

That got my attention.

"What kind of magic powers?" I asked, trying to sound as casual as possible.

"You know," Kenny said. "Like you can travel through time and crap like that."

"Yeah, right," I whispered. "Do you think that if I could travel through time and go to any year in the history of the world, I'd be sitting here listening to *this*?"

Kenny snickered.

The fact is, I *can* travel through time—with baseball cards.

That's not a joke. Ever since I was a little kid, I've had this . . . power, I guess you'd call it. Something strange happened to me whenever I touched an old baseball card. It was a buzzy, vibrating feeling. It didn't hurt, but it was kind of scary. I would drop the card right away, and the tingling sensation would stop.

Then one day, I decided to keep holding on to the card. That buzzy feeling went up my arm and across my body. And the next thing I knew, I was in a different place and a different time. I was in the year 1909 and I met Honus Wagner.

You don't have to believe me if you don't want to. But I know what happened to me. I can do it whenever I want.

What I *didn't* know was how Kenny Cohen found out I could travel through time. I hadn't exactly broadcast the news. I didn't want kids to think I was nuts. Only a few people knew about it. My mom and dad knew. My baseball coach, Flip Valentini, knew. My nine-year-old cousin Samantha knew.

"Yo, Kenny," I whispered, turning around in my seat, "who told you that crap about me?"

"Fuller," he said.

Bobby Fuller! That figured. I should have known. Bobby Fuller has had it in for me ever since I hit a double off him to break up his no-hitter. And that was back in our T-shirt league days! You'd think he would forget about it by the time we got to seventh grade. Bobby Fuller sure could hold a grudge.

In the past few weeks, he had been tormenting me whenever he saw me in the hall or on the ball field. I'm just glad he's not in any of my classes this year.

Some people just rub you the wrong way. Fuller and Kenny were on the same team. They're a couple of prejuvenile delinquents. They should form the Future Inmates of America Club. I'm sure that ten years from now I'll pick up a newspaper and read that the two of them were arrested for something or other.

"Fuller said you were a freak," Kenny whispered. "He said you're an alien disguised as a human. He said he's gonna get you at the game after school today."

"That what he said?" I asked.

"Yeah, are you gonna show?"

"Of *course* I'm gonna show," I said. "Bobby Fuller doesn't scare me."

"Mr. Stoshack! Mr. Cohen!" Mrs. Van Hook suddenly said. "What is so important that you need to discuss it in the middle of my class?"

"Uh, baseball, Mrs. Van Hook," Kenny said.

What an idiot! Any fool knows that when the teacher catches you talking and asks you what you're talking about, you're supposed to say, "Nothing." Kenny Cohen is a moron.

"Baseball?" spat Mrs. Van Hook. "The Civil War was perhaps the most important event in our nation's history. It defined us as a nation. And you're talking about *baseball*? Tell me, do you boys find the Civil War to be boring?"

"Oh no, Mrs. Van Hook!" I said, jumping in before Kenny had the chance to say something stupid like, "Yes."

"Good. Because over the weekend I want you to read Chapter Twenty-six in your textbooks. There will be a test on this material next week."

Everybody groaned, out of habit. As we filed out of the room, Mrs. Van Hook pointed a finger at me and gestured for me to come to her desk.

"Is something wrong at home, Joseph?" she asked once all the other kids had left the room.

Most everybody at school knew that my dad had been in a pretty bad car accident not long ago. Some people had been acting weird toward me, going out of their way to be all nice to make me feel better.

"No," I said. "Everything's fine."

"I don't like what I see, Joseph," said Mrs. Van

Hook. "Your grades have been slipping. You're heading for a C this marking period, maybe even a D. You're a better student than that."

"I'll bring it up, Mrs. Van Hook," I said. "Promise."

D in social studies. Ha! Little did I know that getting a D would be the *least* of my problems.

2

My Good Friend Bobby Fuller

"HEY STOSHACK! ARE YOU NATURALLY STUPID, OR DID IT take a lot of practice? Ha-ha-ha! Hey, is it true that when you go to the zoo, the baboons take pictures of *you*?"

I'm not sure if Bobby Fuller is certified as a psycho, but he should be. Bobby used to pitch, but they switched him over to third base so he couldn't throw at batters' heads anymore. He was shouting at me, using his glove as a megaphone.

I stepped into the batter's box. My team, Flip's Fan Club, was down by a run, and we had come all the way back from 8-1. Kit Clement was on third base, and I really wanted to drive him in and keep the rally going. It was the sixth inning, so this was our last chance.

"Hey Stoshack, you ain't gonna be the hero. You suck, man!"

Fuller used to really get to me. He could make some stupid comment and rattle me just enough to throw off my swing a little so I'd strike out or pop up or something. But he didn't bother me anymore. Now he just seemed pathetic. And the more it didn't bother me, the more it bothered Fuller that it didn't bother me, if you know what I mean. It just made him worse. He figured that if he just got rude enough, eventually he would say something that would get to me.

But he couldn't. I saw a pitch I liked and ripped it down the right field line. It skipped past the first-base bag, and the umpire yelled, "Fair ball!"

I took off. Kit trotted home from third with the tying run, and it occurred to me as I was heading for first that this could be the game. If the ball was misplayed in the outfield, I could make it all the way around and score the winning run. I pushed off the first-base bag with all I had and dug for second.

I couldn't see the right-field corner anymore. But I could hear everybody on our bench screaming, "Go! Go!" so I knew I was going to make a try for third at the very least. If I stopped at third, I knew I could score on a hit, an error, a passed ball, a wild pitch, a sacrifice fly—all kinds of ways.

I looked toward third. Coach Valentini always tells us that when you're rounding second, you shouldn't turn around to see where the ball is. Instead, you should look to the third-base coach. He will signal you to slide, go in standing up, or if you're lucky, he'll windmill his arm around, which means keep going and try for home.

My eye caught Bobby Fuller at third base. If Fuller looked like he was ready to catch the relay from right field, I knew I would have to slide in and try to beat the throw. But he didn't. He was just standing there, his hand on his hip, shaking his head sadly. It looked like he was waiting for a bus or something.

The ball must be still bouncing around the right-field corner, I figured. I would be able to trot home with the winning run, no sweat.

Then I remembered that Fuller might be trying to deke me. If you know baseball, you know that infielders are trained to be masters of deception. They try to fake you out all the time. Fuller could be standing around like that so I would slow down. Then, when the ball approached, he would quickly grab it and slap the tag on me. I do that all the time. When you're running the bases, you should never look at infielders to decide what to do.

Finally I spotted Coach Valentini, who was coaching at third. He was putting both hands down, which is the signal to slide. I hit the dirt.

Just as I had suspected; Fuller suddenly got down into position to receive the throw from right field. The ball skipped once on the infield dirt and short-hopped into Fuller's glove. He smacked the glove against the back of my head just a millisecond after my toe touched third base.

I knew I was safe, but I looked to the umpire anyway. It's not uncommon that they blow the call, at least in my league.

"Safe!" the ump hollered.

"Oh man, I had him!" Fuller protested.

"I said *safe*!" the ump said, staring at Fuller, daring him to argue. "I don't change my calls."

"The man made the call," Coach Valentini said.

As I got up and brushed off my pants, I looked up in the bleachers to see if I could find my mother. Whenever I make a good hit, I want her to see it. But she wasn't there. Maybe she had to work late at the hospital or something, I figured.

My neck was throbbing; Fuller slapped his glove on me harder than he had to. I tried not to rub it. I didn't want him to have the satisfaction of knowing he had hurt me.

Coach Valentini leaned over to congratulate me on the triple, and to make sure I knew the situation. The game was tied now. I represented the winning run on third. One out.

"Okay, you know what to do, Stosh," the coach mumbled. "You're not in a force situation, so you don't have to run. But if you can make it home, we win this thing. So be ready to score. Got it?"

"Got it."

Coach Valentini went to talk the situation over with the batter, Anthony Blengino. He was a decent hitter, but the coach might have been telling him to let a few pitches go by to see if the pitcher would throw one wild. Or maybe he was telling Anthony to drop down a squeeze bunt to bring me home.

"Hey Stoshie," Bobby Fuller said from his third-base position, just loud enough for me to hear.

I ignored him. I didn't need to be distracted by him when I was trying to win the game. I knew he was trying to do something to psych me out. I kicked at the dirt around the third-base bag.

"Yo, Elephant Ears," Fuller said. "I hear you can travel through time."

I stopped kicking at the dirt. I looked at him.

"Who said that?" I asked. How could Bobby Fuller possibly know that I could travel through time?

"I've got my sources," he said, grinning his stupid grin.

Maybe he was bluffing. Maybe he just made up something to be outrageous and it was just an amazing coincidence that it was true. Or maybe he knew.

"Who told you that?" I said, more forcefully.

"My kid sister," he said. "She goes to school with your cousin Samantha. Your cousin said you told her you could travel through time, Stoshack. Ooh, that must be *creepy*." Fuller started making flying saucer noises with his mouth.

Samantha! I knew I shouldn't have been showing off in front of that annoying little runt. She slipped a card into my hand when I was about to go back and meet Mickey Mantle in 1951, and the next thing I knew, it was 1944 and I was sitting in the dugout of an all-girls team in Milwaukee.

Samantha and my aunt had moved to Louisville from Massachusetts recently, and she was nothing but trouble.

Coach Valentini had finished his chat with Anthony and was heading back to the third-base coaching box.

"You're a freak, Stoshack," Fuller whispered. "A mutant. Just wait until I spread the word around school that you think you can travel through time. They'll laugh you right out of town!"

"One out, everybody!" the pitcher shouted. "Let's get this guy."

I was determined to put what Fuller said out of my mind. I wasn't going to let him bother me. I put my toe on third base and focused on the pitcher.

Mentally I went over what I was going to do in any situation. If the pitch got past the catcher, I was going to try to score. If Anthony put a bunt down, I was going to try to score. If he hit a slow roller to anyone but the pitcher, I was going to try to score. If Anthony hit one past the infield on the ground, I was going to try to score. If the ball was hit in the air, I would stop to see if it would be caught. And if it was hit far enough into the outfield, I would tag up and then try to score. If anything *else* happened, I would stay on third and then try to score with the next batter.

Baseball is so complicated. That's why I love it.

"C'mon, Tony," I shouted, clapping my hands. "Drive me in, baby!"

Anthony looked over the first two pitches. They both looked good, but the ump called one a ball and one a strike. Anthony stepped out of the batter's box to look at Coach Valentini. I looked at him too. Our bunt sign was when the coach would say the words "swing away." The coach didn't say it, so I knew Anthony would be swinging away. I took a few steps off the third-base bag.

"You ain't gonna score, Stoshack," Fuller said.

"Let's see you try and stop me," I replied.

On the next pitch, Anthony took a rip and made contact. It was a high fly to left field. I could tell it wasn't going to make it over the fence, but it looked deep enough for me to tag up. The left fielder drifted back. He had it in his sights.

I retreated to third base, putting my foot firmly against the bag. I knew the left fielder had a good arm, so I wanted to take off for home the instant he made the catch.

As soon as the ball settled in his glove, I broke for home. Or I tried to break for home, anyway. Something was holding me back.

Fuller! He had his hand on my belt! That jerk!

He held on for about half a second, not long enough to get caught, but just long enough to slow me down. When I finally broke loose I stumbled, and then started running for home again.

Everybody was shouting, "Slide! Slide!" I knew I

would have to get a toe on the plate before the ball got there or barrel into the catcher and knock the ball loose. With a little luck, the throw would go off line or maybe hit me and bounce away.

No such luck. The throw was right there at about the same time as my foot. I sent a shower of dirt flying, and the catcher put his mitt on my leg. I looked up at the umpire, really not sure if I had beaten the tag or not.

"Yer out!" the ump hollered.

The game was over. They don't play extra innings in our league, so it ended in a tie. As I lay there in the dirt, Bobby Fuller and his teammates mobbed their left fielder, who had made the great throw. My teammates gathered up the bats and balls and stuff and started stuffing them into their duffel bags.

I could have protested. I could have told the ump that Fuller grabbed my belt from behind and prevented me from scoring. But it would have been pointless. The ump said it himself. He didn't change his calls.

As Fuller ran off the field, I glared at him.

"Bet you wish you could travel through time *now*, Stoshack," he said. "Like to five minutes ago! Ha-ha-ha-ha!"

I could hear his stupid laugh all the way from the parking lot.

3

The Guy Who Invented Baseball (Maybe)

COACH VALENTINI GATHERED THE TEAM AROUND HIM IN the dugout. When we were younger, one of the moms or dads would provide snacks after the game. But the coach decided that we were too big for that. He handed each of us a pack of baseball cards to take home with us.

Flip Valentini doesn't *have* to coach our team. He does it for the fun of it. Flip doesn't have to work at all. But he runs Flip's Fan Club, the local baseball-card shop where a lot of us hang out. I doubt that he makes much money doing it. Coaching us and running the store is Flip's idea of being retired. He loves baseball and always tells us he was a pretty decent pitcher in his day. Of course, that was a long time ago. He must be seventy years old now. Maybe older.

Some of the guys were complaining that Bobby

Fuller had cheated, and that's why we didn't win the game. But the coach just put a finger to his lips to quiet them down. I knew he didn't like complainers, so I didn't even tell him what Fuller had done.

"Fuhgetaboutit," Flip told us as he ran his bony hand through his white hair. "Y'know, when I was growin' up in Brooklyn, my team was the Dodgers. 'Dem Bums,' we called 'em. They were a great team, like youse guys. But they lost every stinkin' year to the Yankees in the Series. Every October it was always the same story. Wait till next year, wait till next year. But the Bums never gave up. They was always battlin'."

"And I bet they eventually won the World Series, right, Coach?" asked our second baseman, Gabe Radley. We had all heard enough of Flip's old baseball stories to know where he was going.

"You're darn tootin' they did!" Flip said. "They finally beat them Yanks in '55 and brought Brooklyn the only Series we ever won. And then, two years later, the Dodgers said they were gonna up and leave Brooklyn. They moved to California and became the Los Angeles Dodgers. Big league baseball was gone from Brooklyn, forever. Fuhgetaboutit."

Flip was shaking his head sadly, like the whole thing had happened yesterday.

"What's that got to do with us, Coach?" our right fielder, Burton Ernie, asked. "Are we moving to California?"

Burton is not the brightest bulb in the box. He puts two and two together and comes up with five. Burton's real last name is Johnson, but everybody calls him Burton Ernie because he probably still watches *Sesame Street*. Honestly, I can't imagine how he made it past sixth grade.

"No, you lunkhead! The point is, youse kids should never give up neither. We'll get 'em next time, boys. And we play these creeps again next Thursday, so be ready to battle. Next time *we'll* whup them for sure. Right, Stosh?"

"Right, Coach!" I said.

Flip Valentini cracks me up. He's pretty cool for an old guy. It's hard to imagine him being young, but Flip told us that when he was a kid, he and his friends played a game of flipping baseball cards against a wall. Whoever flipped a card closest to the wall got to keep all the cards. That's how he got the nickname "Flip." We used to be called the Yellow Jackets, but then Flip decided to sponsor us. He liked owning the team so much, he decided to coach us too.

Flip also said he and his friends used to take baseball cards and stick them into the spokes of their bike wheels with clothespins so they would make a sound like a motorcycle.

Can you believe that? Throwing your baseball cards at a wall? Mangling them in your bike spokes? Man, I keep my cards in clear plastic pages that fit into loose-leaf binders. If anybody tried to stick my cards into the spokes of a bike, I'd go crazy.

Those were just different times, I guess.

I've been a card collector for a long time. Baseball, football, hockey, basketball. My dad got me started when I was little. That was before he and my mom split up. Dad still gives me cards sometimes. But mostly I get cards from Flip. I either buy them at his store or he hands them out after our games.

I don't see my own dad very much, so Flip is almost like a father to me.

"Do you guys all have rides home?" Flip asked.

I usually rode my bike home after our games, but my mom had told me she was going to get off work early enough to catch the last few innings and drive me home. She still hadn't shown up, so Flip said he'd be happy to drop me off.

Flip was one of the few people who knew my big secret. What happened was that Flip's landlord had doubled his rent, and Flip told us he was going to have to close the store. That would have been tragic. So I got him some money.

You see, Flip had told me that Shoeless Joe Jackson's autograph was worth half a million dollars, so I went back to 1919 and got Shoeless Joe to sign two pieces of paper for me. I gave them to Flip as a present. At first he thought the autographs were faked, but I convinced him that they were real and that I could really travel through time with baseball cards.

Flip sold one of the autographs, and that saved

the store from going out of business. Flip was always nice to me, but ever since that happened, he would do anything for me.

"He grabbed ya, didn't he?" Flip asked after I'd buckled my seat belt.

"Huh?"

"Bobby Fuller at third base," Flip said. "He must've done somethin' to stop ya from scorin'."

"How did you know, Coach?"

"It took you about an hour to get to the plate!"

"He held on to my belt," I admitted.

Flip threw his head back and laughed. "That Fuller kid is nuts, but I gotta admit it, he's smart. You got to use your noodle to beat guys like that."

It *was* pretty clever, come to think of it.

"So," Flip said, "you doin' any time travelin' recently?"

"I've been playing it cool," I said. "My mom doesn't exactly approve. She thinks it's too dangerous."

"She's right," Flip said. "It is. She's only lookin' out fer ya, Stosh."

It had been a little while since my last "trip." I had already been looking through my baseball card collection, thinking about which player I might go visit next.

"Hey Flip," I said as he pulled up to my house, "if you could travel through time with a baseball card and you could watch anybody in history play, who would you visit? Joe DiMaggio? Ted Williams? Roger Maris?"

Flip pulled up the emergency brake and scratched his head. "That's a toughie," he said. "I seen all those guys play, so it wouldn't be such a big deal. When I was young, I saw all the greats from the 1940s and 1950s."

He wrinkled up his forehead for a moment, and then he brightened.

"There've been a lotta great players over the years," he finally said, "but there *is* one guy I'd really like to meet."

"Who's that?" I asked.

"Abner Doubleday."

"Abner Doubleday?"

I had heard the name. I'd seen it in baseball books, and every so often I'd hear some TV announcer say something like, "Old Abner Doubleday must be turning over in his grave after that bonehead play." But I didn't know who he was.

"Abner Doubleday," Flip continued, "was the guy who invented the game of baseball.

"Oh . . ."

"Or so they say," Flip quickly added. "Some people say he did, and other people say he didn't."

"Why don't they know for sure?" I asked.

"The story goes that Doubleday grew up in Cooperstown, New York—yeah, where the Baseball Hall of Fame is today. And one day—this is 1840 or somethin' like that—he sketched out a baseball diamond in the dirt with a stick outside the local barber shop. He put nine players on each team, three outs, three strikes, yadda yadda yadda, and told the kids how to play this new game. But he never put it on paper and never copyrighted it or nothin'."

"So how did anybody find out?"

"Well, that's the thing. It wasn't till long after Doubleday was dead that one of those kids came forward and said that was the first baseball game. Maybe he was lyin', or maybe he was tellin' the truth. Nobody'll ever know for sure if Doubleday invented baseball or not. That's who *I'd* like to talk to, old Abner Doubleday."

"I could find out!" I said excitedly. "I could go back in time and find out! Maybe I could even watch baseball get invented! How cool would that be?"

Flip snorted. "Only one problem, Stosh," he said. "There's no such thing as an Abner Doubleday baseball card. They didn't even *have* baseball cards back then. End of story."

"Oh," I said, getting out of the car. "Bummer."

"Yeah, I guess we'll never know who invented baseball," Flip said. "Too bad, huh?"

"Yeah."

"Hey Stosh," Flip said before he pulled away from the curb. "Don't let Fuller get you down. We'll figure out a way to beat him next week."

"Okay, Coach."

4

Mom and Uncle Wilbur

WHEN I GOT HOME, I KNEW RIGHT AWAY WHY MOM hadn't made it to my game. She was fast asleep on the couch in the living room.

My mother is a nurse in the emergency room at Louisville Hospital. That's in Kentucky, by the way. Mom works really long and crazy hours. Sometimes she's so exhausted at the end of the day that she just sacks out, still wearing her nurse's uniform.

It's hard on Mom because she has to take care of me and my great-great-uncle Wilbur too. He was sitting across from the couch in his wheelchair. Uncle Wilbur was also sleeping when I came in, but he opened his eyes when I clicked the screen door shut. He smiled at me and gave me the shush sign so I wouldn't wake Mom.

I don't think it's an exaggeration to say that Uncle Wilbur is alive thanks to me.

What happened was that when I went back to 1919 to meet Shoeless Joe Jackson, I also tracked down Uncle Wilbur when he was a kid. Mom had told me that he died from a disease called influenza when he was a boy. I gave him some of the flu medicine I had brought with me, and when I returned to the present day, Uncle Wilbur was *alive*. The medicine I gave him in 1919 saved his life. It was the most amazing thing.

Now Uncle Wilbur is really old. He doesn't do much besides sit around and watch sports on TV.

"Did you win your game?" he whispered.

"Nah," I said. "Tied. I hit a triple, though. I would have tagged up to score the winning run, but the third baseman grabbed my belt and held me back for a second."

"You shoulda beat the crap outta him," Uncle Wilbur said. "That's what I woulda done."

I guess I'm just not the crap-beating type.

Mom opened her eyes. When she saw me standing there in my uniform, she quickly looked at her watch and slapped her forehead.

"Joey!" she said. "I missed your game! Oh, I'm so sorry! I meant to come. I just sat down on the couch to rest for a minute and—"

"It's okay, Mom. Coach Valentini gave me a ride home."

"I'll fix dinner," she said.

"Why, is it broken?" I said to make her laugh, and I went up to my room to change clothes.

As I was peeling off my sweaty uniform, I started thinking about Abner Doubleday. It would be so cool to go back in time to meet him and find out whether or not he really invented baseball.

But how could I do it? Doubleday wasn't a baseball player. There weren't any cards of him. And even if he *had* been a player, there wouldn't have been any cards of him. The first baseball cards, I knew, were printed in 1887. If Doubleday invented baseball around 1840 at the age of, say, twenty, then he had to be over sixty years old in 1887. Too old to play pro baseball.

Mom called me down for dinner, and I told her I would be right there.

There was another reason why there probably couldn't be an Abner Doubleday card, it occurred to me. Baseball cards have photographs on them. It was very possible that photography hadn't even been invented in Doubleday's time.

As Coach Valentini says, end of story.

A *photograph*. An idea started to form in my head.

There used to be an old lady named Amanda Young who lived next door to us. One day she showed me an old photo she had of Honus Wagner, the Pittsburgh Pirate star. I tried to use the photo to send her back to 1909 to meet Honus Wagner. I don't know if it worked, but I will say this—I never saw Amanda Young again. Neither did anyone else. She just vanished off the face of the earth. The

Louisville police are still looking for her.

If I could send Miss Young back through time using a photograph, maybe I could use a photograph of Abner Doubleday to send myself back in time too.

That is, if a photo of Abner Doubleday even existed.

It was certainly worth a shot. There was no harm in trying.

Mom shouted that dinner was getting cold, so I washed my hands and joined her and Uncle Wilbur in the kitchen.

Mom always likes to talk about our day as we eat, no matter how boring it was. I told them about my game. Uncle Wilbur told us about some silly talk show he watches where people argue all the time and start punching each other. Mom told us that one of the patients at the hospital almost died, and they had to give her CPR. That stands for cardiopulmonary resuscitation.

I didn't mention Abner Doubleday. Even if I could find a photograph of him, there was no way Mom was going to let me go meet the guy. She never really approved of my time-travel "foolishness," even after I saved Uncle Wilbur's life. She thinks it's too dangerous.

My mother is a bit of a wimp, if you ask me. She's really tiny, not even five feet tall. I can even pick her up. She worries about every little thing. I think it's because she's so small that she's easily intimidated.

I would bet that if she was bigger, she wouldn't be so overprotective of me. That's my theory, anyway.

In fact, Mom doesn't know the half of it. I almost got killed a few times. If I had ever let Mom know about any of the stuff that happened to me during my time travels, I'd be grounded forever.

But I just tell her the only thing that ever happens is that I get some history lessons. It's *educational*, I always tell her. She loves that stuff.

Still, she's suspicious. I'm sure that if I told her I was going to go back to the nineteenth century to ask Abner Doubleday if he really invented baseball, she'd say no.

I had some math and social studies homework to do, so I excused myself from the table and went upstairs. Most of the stuff was easy, but I had to go online to look up a few things for social studies. Some kids I knew sent me instant messages, and I shot a few back to them.

Abner Doubleday was still in my head. Just for the heck of it, I surfed over to the website for the National Baseball Hall of Fame. My dad had been to Cooperstown when he was a kid, but I've never been there.

I noticed there was a button that allowed you to send an e-mail to the Hall of Fame. I sat there for a long time, holding the cursor over that button. Finally, I decided to click it. This is what I typed . . .

Dear Sirs or Madams,
I am a 13-year-old boy who lives in Louisville, Kentucky. I have been playing baseball since I was little, and I am a big fan too. I was wondering if there exists a photograph of Abner Doubleday, and if so, do you have one and can you send it to me? I am willing to pay up to ten dollars. Any other information you might have about Abner Doubleday would be excellent.

Sincerely,
Joe Stoshack

I added my home address and hit the SEND button. A few of my instant message buddies were trying to reach me again, but before I could write back I heard my mom calling.

"What is it?" I hollered.

"Joey!" Mom yelled upstairs, "Your father is on the phone."

5

Easy Money

MY DAD TAUGHT ME JUST ABOUT EVERYTHING I KNOW. He taught me how to play ball, of course, and all about baseball card collecting. He taught me how to fire a rifle and how to throw a Frisbee, how to play gin rummy and how to put together model cars. When I was little he taught me how to fix my bike. When I got bigger, he taught me how to jack up the car and change a flat tire.

My dad once told me that the night I was born he made a list of all the things fathers should teach their sons. He went down the list and checked off the items one by one as he accomplished them. Even after my parents got divorced, Dad would still come over every week and teach me something from his list.

"Every kid needs to know how to build a campfire," he would say. "Someday you'll grow up and I won't be around to do it for you."

He won't be teaching me much anymore, though. My dad was nearly killed in a car accident with a drunken driver. He's lucky, actually, because he was able to gain back some movement in his upper body after a lot of therapy. He still can't walk, though. Dad and I used to spend hours just throwing a baseball back and forth in front of our house. He can't do that anymore, of course, and he really misses it. So do I.

Mom doesn't usually hang around when she drops me off at Dad's apartment. They get along okay, I suppose. But sometimes the old bad feelings come up and they start to argue.

"I've got something cool to show you, Butch," he said. Dad always calls me Butch.

He waited to make sure Mom was gone and then pulled a baseball out of his pocket. It was in one of those clear plastic cases that prevents you from getting fingerprints on it.

I looked at the ball carefully, turning it around until I could see the signature on the other side . . .

Satchel Paige

"Wow."

I knew a little bit about Paige. He was a star pitcher in the Negro Leagues for a long time. When the major leagues finally opened their doors to black players in the late 1940s, he was pretty old. The Cleveland Indians signed him anyway, and he could still get guys out. He was still pitching in the majors when he was about sixty years old. Now he's in the Hall of Fame.

"How much is this worth?" I asked my dad.

"A couple of hundred," he said. "I got it on eBay for half that."

My dad used to be into collecting baseball cards big time. But he got tired of that hobby and sold off most of his collection so he could start collecting autographed baseballs instead.

Ever since his accident he can't work, so he gets disability checks. They're supposed to pay for food and rent and stuff he needs. But I think he spends a good chunk of it on the Three Bees, as he calls them—beer, blackjack, and baseballs. That's one of the reasons he and my mom split up. She didn't like the way Dad spent their money.

"Hey Dad," I said, handing him back the ball. "Did you ever hear of Abner Doubleday?"

"Sure. He's the guy who invented baseball. Everybody knows that."

"Some people say that's just a myth," I told him.

"I went to the Baseball Hall of Fame once when I was a kid," Dad said. "I remember they had this display case with a beat-up old baseball in it. They said it was the Abner Doubleday Baseball, and that they found it with Abner Doubleday's stuff after he died. That's good enough for me."

The first baseball?

"Well, I was thinking . . ." I started.

At that, Dad got this look in his eye that he gets when he thinks he's come up with a great idea. He looked like he might hop right out of the wheelchair. I'm sure he would have if he could have.

"You're gonna go back in time to meet Abner Doubleday!"

"I don't know if it's going to work," I said, "but it would be cool to find out whether or not he really invented baseball."

"Cool? Forget about cool, Joe!" Dad gushed. "You can make yourself a million dollars easy!"

Dad was always thinking of ways to make a million dollars easy. It had never even occurred to me that I could make money by meeting Abner Doubleday.

"How, Dad?"

"It's simple," he said, holding up his autographed Satchel Paige ball. "You ask him to sign a baseball for you!"

"You think a baseball signed by Abner Doubleday would be worth something?"

"Are you kidding?" Dad said. "You will have in your hand the only baseball in the *world* that was signed by the man who actually invented the game! Remember when Barry Bonds hit his seventy-third homer in 2001? That ball sold for around half a million. A ball signed by Abner Doubleday should be worth twice as much as that. The sky's the limit!"

"I don't know, Dad," I said.

I had never told my dad that I got two Shoeless Joe Jackson autographs when I went back to 1919. If he had known that I gave Flip Valentini a million dollars' worth of autographs, Dad would have gone ballistic. But Flip really needed the money, and I wanted to help him out.

There's probably nothing *illegal* about going back in time and using what you know about the future to make money. But I don't feel comfortable with it. Something about it feels wrong. It's like stealing the answers to a test and getting an A on it without having to study. It's cheating.

"Oh come on, Joe!" my dad said. "It's just *one* baseball. All you have to do is get the guy to sign it. That's not asking a lot. It wouldn't hurt anyone. And think of the payoff! You would be able to buy just about anything in the world, Joe."

I tried to come up with reasons not to do it. I told Dad that I would have to use a photograph, because there were no Abner Doubleday baseball cards.

"So see if you can use a photograph," he said.

I told Dad that Mom would probably not let me travel back through time anyway, because with each trip she was getting more concerned about my safety.

"So don't tell her," Dad whispered. "You're a big boy. Mom doesn't have to know everything you do."

"I don't know, Dad . . ."

"Just think about it," he said. "That's all I ask."

When I got home that night, I went up to my room and thought about it. I had never lied to my mother. Well, maybe once or twice when she asked me if I liked her new dress or a new recipe she was trying out. But that was just so I wouldn't hurt her feelings. That's the *good* kind of lying.

I brushed my teeth, climbed into bed, and

thought about it some more. It would be easy enough to go back and meet Doubleday, get one stupid ball signed, and come home without my mother ever knowing I was gone.

But what if I did that? Then I would have a priceless baseball. If I sold it and I suddenly had millions of dollars, Mom would know I'd gone back in time without getting her permission. And if I didn't sell the ball, there wouldn't be much point in having Doubleday sign it to begin with.

It was hard to sleep. But finally I decided that it was ridiculous to torture myself over this whole thing. There were no Abner Doubleday baseball cards. I didn't even know whether or not a photograph of Abner Doubleday even existed.

Eventually I fell asleep.

6

The Photograph

OKAY, SO A PHOTO OF ABNER DOUBLEDAY *DOES* EXIST.

Here's what happened. I usually look through the mail when I get home from school. I give it to Uncle Wilbur, and he looks through it. Then Mom looks through it when she comes home from work an hour later. But it was Friday, the one day Mom gets home before me.

"Joey, there's a package for you!" she hollered upstairs to me.

I came down to the kitchen, and Mom was holding up a large envelope. She was still in her nurse's uniform. Uncle Wilbur was sitting at the kitchen table. The envelope was addressed to me.

I don't usually get a lot of mail. Just a couple of sports magazines and catalogs, mostly. The return address on the envelope Mom was holding said National Baseball Hall of Fame and Museum.

"Hey, maybe you've been inducted into the Hall of Fame, Joe," Uncle Wilbur joked.

At first I didn't know what was going on. Why would the Hall of Fame be contacting *me*? I had completely forgotten about the e-mail I sent to them a few nights earlier.

"Don't just stand there," Mom said. "Open it."

I tore open the envelope. Inside was a letter that said I owed ten dollars for "One black and white, 8 × 10 photo."

I looked in the envelope again and pulled out the photo. It was a picture of a guy. He was wearing some kind of military uniform. He looked very serious. His curly hair was parted so that almost all of it fell to one side of his head.

Abner Doubleday

"Who's the doofus?" Mom asked.

I knew exactly who it was—the one and only Abner Doubleday. I had to admit, he did look a bit like a doofus.

As I held the photo, I felt something strange. It was that tingling sensation, the feeling I got when I touched old baseball cards.

That was it. I remembered the feeling well. It meant I was about to travel through time! It was going to happen!

I dropped the photo on the table before it was too late. The tingling sensation stopped immediately. The photo landed facedown on the kitchen table. This is what was printed across the back . . .

ABNER DOUBLEDAY, 1863. INVENTOR OF BASEBALL?

"What's going on, Joey?" Mom asked.

I must have had a frightened look on my face. I didn't want to tell her about Doubleday yet. I hadn't prepared what I was going to say to her about it. In the back of my mind, I'd assumed there wouldn't be a photo of Doubleday, so I wouldn't have to deal with it.

I decided to just lay it on the line.

"This guy Abner Doubleday may have invented baseball," I said. "Or maybe he didn't. Nobody knows for sure. I was . . . thinking of traveling through time to find out."

I cringed, waiting for her to tell me it was too dangerous and all that.

Mom picked up the picture and turned it over to look at the front of it again. Then she looked at me.

"I think it's a great idea!" she said.

I couldn't believe what I was hearing. All the other times I'd told her I wanted to take one of my "trips," she'd come up with every possible reason why I shouldn't.

"You're kidding, right?" I asked.

"I am not," she said. "I think you should do it."

"You're going to let me go back to 1863?"

"You can go on one condition," she said.

Here it comes, I thought. She's going to make me bring along my boots or cough medicine or something really dorky that will totally embarrass me.

"You have to take *me* with you," Mom said.

I shook my head. I couldn't have heard that right. It was time to get my hearing checked.

"Funny, Mom."

"I want to go," Mom stated. "Whenever you travel through time, I just sit home and worry. You're out there meeting these big celebrities and having these incredible experiences. You get to witness history as it's happening. This has been so educational for you. I guess I've come around to thinking that these trips are a good thing. I want to see what it's like."

Educational? Ha! My mother is clueless.

I'd never told Mom how educational it was when I went to meet Jackie Robinson in 1947 and a psychotic batboy chased me through the streets of Brooklyn, swinging a baseball bat at my head.

I'd never told her how educational it was when I went to meet Shoeless Joe Jackson in 1919 and these gangsters kidnapped me, locked me in a closet, tied me to a chair, and shot at me.

I'd never told Mom that something has gone wrong every trip back through time. History isn't educational. It's history. And a couple of times, I was almost history too!

"Time travel isn't an exact science, Mom," I explained delicately. "It's not like in the movies. You don't step inside some booth, twist a few dials, and *poof*, you're standing next to Babe Ruth or Mickey Mantle. It's not that easy."

"Oh come on, Joey," she said, pinching my cheek. "Working at the hospital is so boring. I need a little adventure in my life. When's the last time we went on a vacation together, anyway?"

"A long time ago."

"Look," she said, her eyes lighting up, "we'll zip back to 1863, ask this Doubleday guy if he invented baseball, and zip right back home. It will take five minutes. We'll have fun. Hey, I'll pack a lunch! We can even have a picnic in the past! What do you think?"

"Uh, I don't know, Mom. What about Uncle Wilbur?"

"He'll be fine." Uncle Wilbur had fallen asleep in his wheelchair. "He'll never even know we were gone."

The whole thing sounded like a bad idea to me. I

mean, I did want to go back in time again. But I didn't particularly want to go with my *mother*. I mean, I'm thirteen years old! I don't even like to be seen going to the supermarket with my mother. Why would I want to travel one hundred and fifty years with her?

"It's dangerous," I said. "You might get hurt."

"Don't worry about me," she said. "Why should you get to have all the fun?"

She wouldn't give it a rest. She kept egging me on, saying I was a party pooper and that I had no spirit of adventure. It was a total role reversal. She was trying to talk *me* into traveling through time, and I was giving *her* all the reasons why it was a bad idea.

"You took your father," she finally said, looking a little hurt.

That was true. I'd taken my father with me to 1932 to see if Babe Ruth really predicted his famous "called shot" home run. I was nearly killed on that trip when I got into a car with the Babe and found out he drove like a maniac. But I never told Mom that.

"Okay, okay," I agreed. "I'll take you with me."

"Yippee!" She looked so happy. "So how do we do it?"

There were two crucial things I needed to bring with me on a trip to meet Abner Doubleday. First, I needed a new pack of cards. Baseball cards take me to the year on the card, so they would be our return ticket home. If I didn't have new cards with me, Mom and I would be stuck in the past forever.

Second, I needed a baseball so I could get it autographed for my dad. And a Sharpie marker, of course, to write on the baseball.

I had Mom take the picture of Doubleday and follow me into the living room. We sat on the couch side by side.

"Oh, wait a minute," she said. "There are a few things I need to bring along too."

She grabbed her purse and ran back to the kitchen, then ran upstairs while I waited. Finally she came back down and sat on the couch next to me.

"What's in the purse?" I asked.

"A first aid kit," she said, going through the bag, "peanut butter crackers. Go-Gurt. A couple of juice boxes. Some other snacks. Medicine. A portable umbrella . . ."

"Do you really have to bring an *umbrella*?" I asked. "You'll look like Mary Poppins with that thing."

"Don't be silly. It might be raining in 1863!"

"You know, there may be a weight limit on how much we can bring along," I said. "Like on a plane."

"Oh, stop it," Mom said. "This weighs next to nothing. Let's go. I don't want to keep Mr. Doubleday waiting for lunch."

"Mom, did it ever occur to you that Abner Doubleday might not *want* to have lunch with us?"

"Then we'll have a picnic without him," my

mother replied. "We don't need that doofus to have a good time."

I took my mother's hand. It had been a long time since we'd held hands. I picked up the photo of Abner Doubleday.

"Are you scared?" I asked her.

"A little," she said, "but scared in a good way."

"Close your eyes, Mom."

It wasn't long until I started to feel a very faint tingling sensation in my fingertips. It was sort of like the feeling you get when you touch a TV screen. It didn't hurt. It was a pleasant feeling. The familiar tingling got stronger, and then my whole hand was vibrating, then my wrists, and then my arms.

"Do you feel it, Mom?" I asked.

"Yes!" she said excitedly.

I felt the sensation sweep across my chest to the other side of my body, then down my legs. I wanted to open my eyes, but I didn't dare because I thought it would be creepy to see myself disappear.

My entire body was tingling now. I had reached the point of no return. I didn't know what would happen if I dropped the picture at this point, and I wasn't about to find out.

At the last possible instant, I grabbed the stupid umbrella from my mother's hand and tossed it aside.

And then we faded away.

7

A Horrible Symphony

I DIDN'T NEED TO OPEN MY EYES TO SEE WHAT WAS going on. I could see it with my eyes closed.

A gigantic yellow-orange ball of fire flashed over my head, brighter and louder than anything I had ever seen produced by Hollywood. This was followed by a booming explosion that knocked me to my knees.

I thought the world had ended. That's how loud it was.

For maybe half a second, I looked around. Mom was still next to me. We were outside, in a cemetery. Or at least there were some tombstones scattered around haphazardly.

It was daytime, but I couldn't see much sky. I couldn't see much of anything beyond ten yards or so. There was a blanket of smoke hanging over the area. It was very hot out. It had to be summertime, I guessed.

There was another flash and explosion, even brighter, louder, and closer than the first one. The blades of grass around me were pushed down in waves, like the ripples in a pond after you throw a stone in the water.

Suddenly stuff was flying all over us. Dirt. Clumps of mud. Sticks, grass, rocks, pieces of tree bark.

It was like we were caught in the middle of a tornado. But this stuff wasn't swirling around, the way I'd imagine a tornado must throw stuff around. It was just flying every which way.

This was no earthquake or volcano or hurricane. No, nature couldn't produce this kind of violence. Somebody was *shooting* at us.

"Hit the dirt!" I shouted to Mom. She didn't need to be told. We each hunkered down behind a tombstone.

There were more explosions, some of them in the distance and some of them just a few yards away. I could hear popping sounds too. Bullets. They sounded like microwave popcorn, if you were inside the microwave oven, maybe inside the bag.

Mom was shouting something to me, but I couldn't hear her over the explosions.

"What?" I screamed.

"Are you okay?" she hollered.

Am I okay?! Oh yeah, bombs were exploding all around us. Stuff was flying. I could die any second, and Mom wanted to know if I was *okay*.

Sure, I was okay. This was like going for a walk in the park. Too bad I didn't bring that stupid umbrella. It might rain.

A bullet whizzed past my ear. I felt it as it went by. The bullet chipped off a little piece of the tombstone I was hiding behind. One more inch and it would have chipped off a piece of my head.

"Stay down!" I screamed, as if saying that was really necessary.

I was lying on my stomach in the dirt now, trying my best to press my body flat against the ground. Mom was doing the same thing. I could smell something in the air. Gunpowder. Sulfur, maybe. Something burning.

"Where are we?" Mom screamed.

"How should I know?"

"Well, you've done this before, haven't you?"

"It's never been like this!"

I had no idea where I was or *when* I was. But I did know that I didn't want to be here.

I tried to curl myself into a ball so I would take up the smallest possible surface area. I wanted to minimize the chances of one of those flying pieces of who-knows-what finding a part of me.

"We've got to get out of here!" Mom shouted.

No fooling. I tried to reach into my pocket to get out my new pack of baseball cards, so we could go back home.

Bang bang, pop pop pop, bang bang BOOM. They were coming faster now. It was a symphony of noises. Horrible noises. I could feel the explosions in my chest. My ears hurt. The ground was vibrating. Bullets were flying all around me. I felt the air, the hiss the bullets made as they zipped by.

What was going on? This could not be happening. Maybe it was a bad dream or something. A hallucination. Maybe I would wake up in a few minutes and I'd be back home. I felt like I was thinking in slow motion.

I was sweating all over. I could feel it dripping under my arms. My shirt was soaked.

A little white rabbit ran by us, looking terrified. At least it had the courage to run for it.

I wanted to cover my ears with my hands to block out the noise of the explosions, but my hands were already covering the top of my head and I didn't want to move them.

It probably wouldn't have mattered anyway. There was no getting around the sound. The pounding was vibrating the ground like rumbling thunder. A patch of dry grass was on fire near me.

Was somebody dropping bombs on us? I didn't hear the sound of airplanes. I didn't hear the sound of anything except explosions and bullets.

"Where's Abner Doubleday?" I thought I heard Mom say, though I couldn't be sure.

Abner Doubleday? I had forgotten all *about* Abner Doubleday. Who cared about Abner Doubleday? All I cared about was staying alive and protecting my mother.

How could I have put her in this situation? I should have stood up to her when she said she wanted to go back in time with me. Too late for that now. I had to deal with the situation we were in.

"Something must have gone wrong!" I shouted back at her.

"No kidding!"

I'm sure my mother had thought we would just drift peacefully back to 1863, like in a dream. We would open our eyes and be sitting in Abner Doubleday's parlor at some fancy tea party. There would be people in old-time clothes playing violins and harpsichords, and people outside playing croquet. Like in those boring movies Mom likes so much.

I could taste dirt in my mouth. It was in my nose and ears too. It was in my hair, my clothes, my shoes.

There was a bullet lodged in the dirt a few inches from my head. I plucked it out of the ground to look at it. It didn't look like a modern bullet. It almost looked like it was made of rough stone, with a point and four or five little ridges going around it.

"Watch out, Joey!" Mom shouted.

She was pointing off to the left. I looked that way just in time to see a horse charging toward me. There was no time to react. It was going to trample me. I closed my eyes and tensed every muscle in my body for the impact.

I didn't die. When I opened my eyes, I saw the horse galloping off into the woods. It must have jumped over me.

Somewhere in the distance, I could swear I heard the sound of a trumpet. I couldn't see anything. Smoke was everywhere, and I was keeping my head down. Whoever was out there, they sure didn't like us.

I didn't have time to wonder about such things because at that instant something smashed into a tree behind me with a thud. It might have been a cannonball.

There was a long, slow cracking noise, like a creaky door opening. I turned around to see the tree splitting down the middle. One side was coming down, and it was falling in our direction.

"Watch out, Mom!" I hollered.

Instinctively, we both rolled to our left. The tree trunk slammed down right where we had been lying. It pushed the tombstone I was hiding behind into the ground like a hammer driving in a nail with one blow.

Mom and I huddled against the tree trunk, and against each other. The tree was better protection than the tombstones.

The bombardment went on and on. I didn't know how long. I lost all concept of time. Maybe it was five minutes, maybe half an hour.

It was a miracle that we hadn't been hit. Or maybe one of us *had* been hit and didn't even know it. How would I know? The worst injury I ever had was a sprained ankle. For all I knew, you didn't feel anything when a bullet hit you. But I didn't feel any excruciating pain anywhere, I'll say that much.

More explosions. More bullets. When would it end? This couldn't go on forever. Whoever was shooting at us would have to run out of ammunition at some point.

A piece of paper blew over and got stuck on the tree trunk. I reached out to grab it.

Suddenly I realized what was going on. The date on it was June 1863.

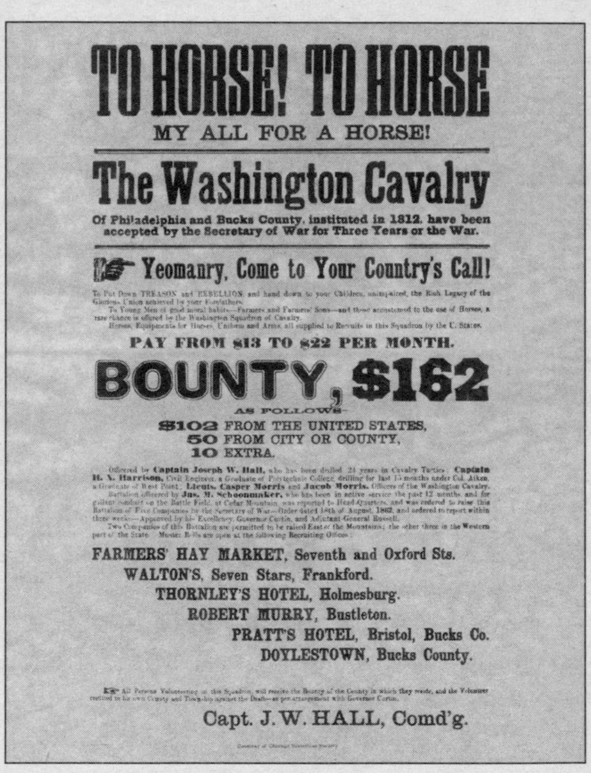

TO HORSE! TO HORSE

MY ALL FOR A HORSE!

The Washington Cavalry

Of Philadelphia and Bucks County, instituted in 1812, have been accepted by the Secretary of War for Three Years or the War.

Yeomanry, Come to Your Country's Call!

To Put Down TREASON and REBELLION, and hand down to your Children, unimpaired, the Rich Legacy of the Glorious Union achieved by your Forefathers.

To Young Men of good moral habits—Farmers and Farmers' Sons—and those accustomed to the use of Horses, a rare chance is offered by the Washington Squadron of Cavalry.

Horses, Equipments for Horses, Uniform and Arms, all supplied to Recruits in this Squadron by the U. States.

PAY FROM $13 TO $22 PER MONTH.

BOUNTY, $162

AS FOLLOWS

$102 FROM THE UNITED STATES,
50 FROM CITY OR COUNTY,
10 EXTRA.

Officered by **Captain Joseph W. Hall**, who has been drilled 23 years in Cavalry Tactics; **Captain H. N. Harrison**, Civil Engineer, a Graduate of Polytechnic College, drilling for last 15 months under Col. Aiken, a Graduate of West Point; **Lieuts. Casper Morris** and **Jacob Morris**, Officers of the Washington Cavalry.

Battalion officered by **Jas. M. Schoonmaker**, who has been in active service the past 12 months, and for gallant conduct on the Battle Field, at Cedar Mountain, was reported to Head-Quarters, and was ordered to raise this Battalion of Five Companies by the Secretary of War—Order dated 18th of August, 1862, and ordered to report within three weeks—Approved by his Excellency, Governor Curtin, and Adjutant-General Russell.

Two Companies of this Battalion are permitted to be raised East of the Mountains; the other three in the Western part of the State. Muster Rolls are open at the following Recruiting Offices:

FARMERS' HAY MARKET, Seventh and Oxford Sts.
WALTON'S, Seven Stars, Frankford.
THORNLEY'S HOTEL, Holmesburg.
ROBERT MURRY, Bustleton.
PRATT'S HOTEL, Bristol, Bucks Co.
DOYLESTOWN, Bucks County.

All Persons Volunteering in this Squadron, will receive the Bounty of the County in which they reside, and the Volunteer credited to his own County and Township against the Draft—as per arrangement with Governor Curtin.

Capt. J. W. HALL, Comd'g.

"Mom," I said, "I think this is the Civil War!"

"Gee, ya think?" she said sarcastically.

How could I have been so dumb? I knew I was sending us back to 1863. Mrs. Van Hook had taught us about the Civil War in social studies. I might not have paid all that much attention, but I knew it began in 1861, and it was the bloodiest war in American history. It never occurred to me that I might send us right into the middle of it.

There was a merciful second or two when there were no explosions. I took the risk of raising my head a few inches over the tree trunk to see what I could see.

There was a flag attached to the tree trunk. It looked like an American flag, except that it didn't have as many stars as a regular flag. Well, that made sense. There are fifty stars for fifty states, and they didn't have fifty states in 1863. I wasn't going to bother counting them.

The flag was ripped. Bullets had torn through it in a bunch of places.

"The flag, Mom!" I shouted. "They're not shooting at *us*! They must be shooting at the *flag*."

There was another explosion in the air over our heads, and stuff showered down around us. I wrapped my arms around Mom to shield her.

Maybe if I took the flag and threw it as far away as possible, they would stop shooting at us. But I couldn't reach the flag. I wasn't about to go get it, either.

If I couldn't get rid of the flag, I'd have to get rid of *us*.

"Mom!" I shouted in her ear. "We've got to make a run for it."

"Are you out of your mind, Joey? We'll get killed!"

"We've got no chance if we stay here," I shouted at her. "Eventually we're going to get hit."

"I'm staying right here!" my mother said. "And so are you."

A couple of bullets thwacked into the tree trunk, inches from our heads.

"We're going to get killed if we stay here!" I shouted. "We've got to get away from the flag."

"No!"

There was no arguing with her. She's my mother. I can't tell her what to do. So I did the only thing I could do, the only thing that made any sense to me in the situation.

I scooped up my mother in both arms and made a run for it.

8

The Firestorm

"ARE YOU CRAZY?" MY MOTHER SCREAMED IN MY EAR AS I carried her across the cemetery.

I didn't know where I was going. I didn't know what I was going to do. I just wanted to get the two of us away from that flag before we got killed.

My mother is skinny. She weighs about a hundred pounds. I know that because she's constantly telling me, "I have to go on Weight Watchers. I'm a hundred pounds. I'm so fat." Women are always complaining about how fat they are, even if they are skinny. It felt like I was carrying a feather. Bullets, explosions, and bombs going off all around have a way of distracting you from minor inconveniences, like trying to run through a graveyard while carrying a one-hundred-pound woman.

I almost tripped over a bunch of tree roots. Something landed ten yards to the left of me and exploded when it hit the ground. I kept running. If we were going to get killed, there was nothing I could do about it. I had to make a run for it.

I was looking around frantically for a place for us to hide from the explosions. The smoke was thick. It was hard to see very far in any direction.

"Over there!" Mom shouted, pointing at a ditch about twenty yards to the right. A stone house would have been my preference, but I couldn't be choosy. I ran over to where she pointed, and we just about dove into the ditch.

"Are you okay?" I asked her.

"I think so."

Mom checked to see if there were any bullet holes in my clothing. Not finding any, she checked herself. Her nurse's uniform was caked with dirt, but no blood. Explosions were still going off, but they weren't right next to us anymore.

"We've got to get out of here, Mom," I said. "I made a big mistake."

"Get out your baseball cards," she said hurriedly.

I was fumbling around in my pockets to dig out the cards that would take us home, when I sensed that somebody was looking at me. Sometimes you just know that somebody is looking at you.

I looked up. We weren't alone in the ditch.

There were four guys staring at us. Their mouths were open, like they couldn't believe what they were looking at.

They had to be Union soldiers. I had seen

enough Civil War movies and pictures to recognize the blue uniforms. These guys didn't look much older than me. Their faces were black from gunpowder, dust, and dirt. Each of them had a long rifle in his hands, and one of them had a snare drum.

Little John

"Who in thunderation are *you*?" one of the boys finally asked. He was the tallest one, and probably the oldest. He had a thin beard. I noticed he had no shoes on.

"I'm Joe Stoshack," I said, sticking out my hand. "Most people call me Stosh. And this is my mother."

"Pleased to meet you," Mom said, brushing dirt off herself.

"You brought your *mother*?"

This came from a little guy, even shorter than me. He was the one with the drum.

"How did you get here?" asked the third one, a blond-haired boy.

"We, uh . . . got a little lost," I said.

"Let's just shoot 'em," the fourth boy said. "They may be Rebs."

"Shut your mouth, Willie," said the tall one, who seemed to be in charge.

"We're not Rebs!" I said, raising my hands to show I didn't have a weapon. I remembered from social studies that the Confederates in the Civil War were called Rebels.

The tall kid told us his name was Joshua, and that they were all part of the 151st Pennsylvania. The short guy with the drum said his name was Little John, and the blond kid's name was Rufus. We shook hands all around, except for that Willie guy who had said he wanted to shoot us.

"Stand around squawkin' all you want," Willie said. "But I'm here to shoot Rebs."

Willie positioned himself at the edge of the ditch and put his gun to his shoulder. But before he could pull the trigger, a bullet slammed into him. He spun around and fell backward against the back wall of the ditch.

"They got Willie!" Joshua shouted.

The other three gathered around Willie trying to help him, but he was screaming out from the pain, yelling, "Don't touch me! Don't take me to the doctor!

Just let me die here!" He was holding his shoulder, and I could see blood on his hands.

Mom rushed over and knelt down next to Willie, taking his head in her hands. He was looking dazed and confused, like he might black out.

"Can you tell me your name?" she asked him. "Do you know where you are?"

"Willie Biddle," he said, gritting his teeth. "I'm in Gettysburg, Pennsylvania. Just let me die!"

Mom and I looked at each other. We were at the Battle of Gettysburg! I didn't know much about it, but I knew it was probably the most famous battle of the Civil War.

"You're going to be okay," she assured Willie. "I'm a nurse. I can help you. You're not going to die."

"No doctor!" Willie screamed. "Promise me you won't get the doctors."

"Shhhh," Mom said. "Let me have a look at this."

Mom ripped off Willie's sleeve, and it was a bloody mess. Joshua, Little John, and Rufus turned away. So did I. Open wounds have never been my favorite thing to look at.

"I'm glad I brought along a first aid kit," Mom told Willie. "I'll have you patched up in no time."

"Ma'am," Willie grunted, "I'm sorry I said we should shoot you and your boy."

"Don't mention it," Mom said.

While Mom tended to Willie's wounds, Joshua picked up his rifle. Little John and Rufus picked up theirs too. I could still hear gunshots and explosions, but they were mostly in the distance.

"Must've been a stray bullet that got Willie," Joshua said. "But the Rebs could be makin' another charge any minute. We better be ready for 'em."

"What about *him*?" Little John asked. "We need every man we got."

They all looked at me.

"Can you shoot?" Joshua asked me. "Do you know how to handle a rifle?"

"Yeah, but I, uh . . . don't have a gun," I said. "I don't even have a uniform."

"We'll fix you up," Joshua said. He led me over to the other end of the ditch, where, I noticed for the first time, there was another soldier. He was lying against the side of the wall, his eyes closed.

"This is Alexander," Joshua said, pulling a pipe out of his pocket and sticking it in his mouth. "Don't think him rude if he don't shake your hand. He can't on account of he's dead. We'll bury him later. But I reckon he won't be needing his rifle no more. He won't mind if you take it."

I had never seen a dead body before. Alexander was just lying there. It looked like he was asleep. His body wasn't riddled with bullets or anything. He looked so peaceful, like he was about to wake up any second, stretch out his arms, and ask the others what went on while he was napping.

Joshua filled his pipe with some tobacco he scooped out of a pouch, and then he lit it.

"Smoking is bad for you," I advised him.

Alexander looked like he was asleep.

Joshua took a puff on his pipe and glanced over at Alexander sitting in the ditch.

"Sure didn't do him no good," he said.

Little John turned away as Joshua and Rufus took off Alexander's uniform and gave it to me. It wasn't a perfect fit, but it would do. I slipped the baseball out of my pocket and put it into the pocket of the uniform.

"You know how to shoot a Springfield, Stosh?" Joshua asked, handing me the dead boy's rifle.

"Not exactly . . ."

Before his accident, my dad taught me how to

shoot a gun. It was an old .22 caliber Remington. He used to take me out to a field near our house for target practice. We'd shoot at cans and bottles and stuff. I was pretty good. Mom never approved of my firing guns. It was one of the many things Dad liked to do that she didn't approve of.

The Springfield was as tall as I am, and I'm over five and a half feet now. Joshua handed it to me, and it was heavy, maybe ten pounds. He slung a leather bag around my neck that looked a little like a lady's purse. Joshua called it a "shot bag."

"You got twenty cartridges in here," he said.

Joshua took one cartridge out. It was about the size of a Chap Stick, and it was wrapped in paper. He put the tip of the cartridge in his mouth, bit it off, and spit the paper on the ground. Then he poured some black stuff—gunpowder, I figured—out of the cartridge and down the barrel of the gun.

"This is your minié ball," he said, holding up a bullet, which was also inside the paper cartridge. He dropped it into the barrel on top of the powder.

"This is your ramrod," he said, taking a long, thin piece of metal that had been attached to the barrel of the gun. It had a little round thing on one end. Joshua slipped the ramrod into the barrel of the gun and shoved it in there like a plunger two or three times to push the bullet and powder down as far as they would go.

"That's all there is to it," Joshua said, handing me the rifle. "Now you're ready to shoot some Rebs."

Unbelievable! This gun shot just one bullet at a time. It had taken Joshua at least twenty seconds to load the thing. Once it was fired, I'd have to go through the whole procedure all over again.

I just assumed soldiers always fought wars with machine guns, which can fire hundreds of rounds a minute when you pulled the trigger once. I had to remind myself that this was 1863. No high-tech stuff. No helicopters. No night-vision goggles. No laser-guided smart bombs or drones. The Civil War was a bunch of guys—kids, even—running around with single-shot rifles. They didn't even have shields, armor, or helmets.

Heck, the telephone wasn't even invented yet.

"If your aim is true," Joshua said after he handed me the rifle, "you can take down a man from a hundred yards or more."

I took the gun hesitantly. I had never fired a gun at a person before. In fact, I had been carefully trained to never even *point* a gun anywhere near a person. I didn't want to shoot at people. It didn't seem right. I didn't know if I could do it. I hoped I wouldn't have to.

Mom was still tending to Willie Biddle, dressing his wounds and so forth. I went over to Little John, the short one with the drum. He told me we had good position, dug into this ditch and up on a hill where we could look down on the Confederates. John wiped some mud off his drum.

"What's the drum for?" I asked him.

Little John looked at me like I was stupid. "Well, I'm a drummer boy, ain't I?"

"So what do you do with the drum?"

"It's so the general can signal the men what to do," he said. "Say, you ain't never been in a battle before, have you?"

"No. Why doesn't the general just *tell* them what to do?"

"Can't always hear," Little John replied. "It gets pretty loud out here."

I didn't see anybody around who looked like a general. I guessed that the 151st Pennsylvania was scattered across the cemetery in the fighting and these four guys found themselves in this ditch. Some of the smoke had cleared from the field now. I could see off into the distance.

Little John told me he knew about ten different drum calls. There's a drumbeat that means "march," and a drumbeat that means "left face," and another drumbeat that means it's time to eat. I asked him to play me a few of them, but he said he couldn't because it might confuse the soldiers.

"Why do you have to carry a gun if you're the drummer?"

"It ain't my gun," he said matter-of-factly. "I took it off a dead man. Like he said, we need every man we got."

Suddenly, a shrieking, high-pitched scream came out of the distant woods. It sounded like a wounded animal.

"What's that?" I asked, turning to look for the source of the sound. The hairs on my arm were standing up.

"The Rebel yell," Little John said, putting down his drum and picking up his rifle.

"Here they come again!" shouted Joshua.

In the distance, a long line of men started to appear. There were maybe a thousand of them, coming out of the woods. They were walking toward us.

"Hold your fire," Joshua said calmly, aiming his gun. "Don't use up any ammunition until they get close."

"What should I do?" I asked Little John.

"Wait till he gives the word," he advised. "Then fire at anything gray."

The army marching toward us was still very far away, but I could make out Confederate flags and men on horses. To the sides of me, Union soldiers were rushing out from behind trees and tombstones to get into position. Some were wheeling cannons out of the woods.

The Confederates were coming closer, and I could see that they were trotting now.

"Fire!" somebody shouted, and a blast of guns erupted on the left and right of me. A few Confederate soldiers stumbled and fell. The others kept right on coming, pulling together to fill in the holes left by the men who had fallen.

"Keep low! Keep low! Stay alert!" shouted Joshua as he rushed to reload his rifle.

The Confederates stopped for a moment to aim and shoot. A few bullets zipped by. I ducked down into the ditch.

As the Confederates got closer, I could see that only some of them were wearing military uniforms. Most were in tattered old clothes. Few of them had shoes. Some of them had rags wrapped around their feet.

I couldn't pull the trigger.

"What's the matter?" Joshua demanded after firing his second shot. "Is your gun jammed?"

"No."

"Then fire that thing!"

"I . . . don't know if I can . . ."

"Are you an American?"

"Yes."

"Well, then *fight* like an American!"

They were getting closer, and then they were running toward us, screaming that horrible Rebel yell the whole time.

I didn't want to shoot. I didn't want to hit a human being. But there were human beings running toward us and they wanted to hit me. So I pulled the trigger. A yellow-blue flash shot out of the end of the musket, and I was rocked backward.

I didn't know if I hit anything. I rushed to reload.

"Joey!" Mom yelled from the bottom of the ditch. She was still helping Willie. "What are you doing?"

"Protecting you!" I shouted. "Stay down!"

It was a firestorm. Even though each man could

only shoot once every twenty seconds, the roar of gunfire was continuous. There were thousands of us.

Union cannons were booming too. I always thought they just fired cannonballs. But as I was reloading, I could see men shoving these big cans down the barrels of a cannon. Then, when it was fired, stuff sprayed out of the cannon in all directions. It was like a giant shotgun, spitting out death.

One well-aimed blast would take out five guys or even more. I saw a guy fly ten feet in the air after getting hit. I could see men getting their arms or legs blown right off. Still they kept coming.

A shell hit the ground at the base of a boulder and sent it flying about fifteen feet in the air. It came down right on top of a guy. He never knew what hit him. It was horrible.

For a second, I wondered what was happening back home in Louisville. Kids were going to school, playing ball, watching TV, living their lives. Here at Gettysburg, guys not much older than me were shooting and killing each other.

Man, my life was so easy, it occurred to me. We've got a nice house, a car. We turn on the faucet and water comes out. Flip on the switch and the lights turn on. When I'm hungry, I go to the refrigerator and grab something to eat. I'll never complain about anything, ever again, I promised myself. Just get me home safely.

I kept loading and firing, even though I wasn't

always sure what I was firing at. My hand was so wet with sweat that I had trouble pushing the ramrod down the gun. The barrel was getting too hot to touch. I had used up most of my cartridges. I kept firing anyway. I didn't know what I was doing. I was insane.

"Fix bayonets!" shouted a guy on horseback.

A two-foot bayonet was attached to the barrel of each rifle. Joshua, Little John, and Rufus snapped their bayonets off and clamped them on to the end of the barrel so the sharp end was pointing out. I watched what they were doing and put my bayonet on too.

"You stand alone between the Rebel army and your homes!" shouted the guy on the horse. He had to be one of the Union generals. "Fight like hell!"

Joshua, Little John, and Rufus got ready to climb out of the ditch.

"Charge!" yelled the general.

I was about to climb out of the ditch when a hand pulled the back of my shirt, and I fell backward.

"Where do you think *you're* going?" Mom said.

"I've got to go defend my country!"

"You stay right here, young man, and defend *me*."

I had to watch. The two armies were right on top of each other now. There was no time to load rifles. They were running around the tombstones in hand-to-hand combat. It looked like professional wrestling, but it was real, they had real weapons, and they were really trying to kill each other.

They were swinging their rifles at each other now, and stabbing each other with bayonets. Men were cursing, cheering, screaming, moaning, and dying. Bugles were blowing. Horses were bolting. The smells of gunpowder and sweat and blood were in the air.

I remember I had once seen one of those Civil War reenactments where guys wearing Union and Confederate uniforms pretended to fight each other. Compared to this, that was like watching a ballet.

I wished I could just blow a whistle and make everything *stop*, like a referee at a hockey game. I wanted to tell them all to knock it off and go sit in the penalty box. I wanted to remind them that they were all Americans who spoke the same language and who loved their country.

It was useless, of course. The only thing that would stop this fight was if one side gave up.

Finally, that's what happened. The soldiers in gray realized they weren't going to take control of Cemetery Ridge. At least not today. The Union soldiers had better equipment. They had better position. They had more men. And they were defending their own turf.

I never heard anybody yell, "Retreat!" Maybe there was a bugle call or a signal from a drummer boy. But all at once, the soldiers in gray stopped fighting and started to fall back. They didn't run away. They walked away defiantly. It seemed important to them not to be seen running away.

I thought the Union soldiers would chase the Rebels down the hill and fire at their backs, but they didn't.

Suddenly, for the first time since I had arrived, the guns on both sides were completely quiet. It was like somebody had flipped a switch from ON to OFF.

For a moment, the only sound I could hear was my own breathing.

9

Dinner at Gettysburg

WHEN IT WAS ALL OVER, I HATE TO ADMIT IT, I FELT *great*.

I don't know if it's adrenaline or some other chemical that rushes through your body in times of stress, but whatever it was made me feel really alive. It was like all my senses were heightened. I had never felt this way before.

I had survived. I hadn't realized it at first, but Mom and I were holding on to each other for dear life. We had been standing in the ditch watching the end of the battle, our arms around each other. I could feel our hearts beating. We were okay. We didn't let go of each other for a long time.

After a few minutes, Little John walked slowly back to the ditch. Joshua was behind him, carrying the other guy, Rufus, over his shoulder.

"Is he hurt?" I asked.

"He's dead," Little John said, and then he burst into tears. Mom held him as he sobbed.

"We made them Rebs pay for this," said Joshua, lowering Rufus gently to the ground. "I got me four or five of 'em myself."

"They'll be back," said Willie, now bandaged up and on his feet. "Tomorrow, for sure."

They stood around for a minute looking at poor Rufus. He had been shot up pretty good.

I had to turn away. I was not used to death. My grandmother died when I was little, but I didn't go to the funeral because my mother thought I was too young. Joshua, Willie, and Little John had probably seen a lot of death in their lives.

All around us, I could hear the sounds of shovels sticking into dirt, holes being dug. Joshua got out a shovel and started digging on one side of the ditch. I didn't have to ask what he was doing. I knew he was digging graves for Rufus and Alexander, the guy whose uniform I was wearing.

Little John was sniffling and wiping his face on his sleeve as if he had a cold, but it was pretty obvious that he was still crying. He didn't look much older than me. He couldn't have been more than sixteen or seventeen, I figured.

"How old are you?" I asked, after he had pulled himself together.

"Fifteen years," he said.

"They let you join the army at fifteen?"

"Course not," he said. "They took my brother, and

he was eighteen. So I come along too, and they took me. They ain't too picky when you know how to drum and such."

Little John told me that all four of them had lied their way into the army. Rufus was only sixteen and Joshua and Willie were just seventeen.

Things were so different in the 1800s, I thought. Nowadays, there's a record of everything. Birth certificates, Social Security numbers, driver's licenses. Everything is on computer. If I ever tried to pass myself off as eighteen, I'd get caught in a minute. But during the Civil War if a kid looked like he might be anywhere near eighteen, he could get away with it. Why anybody would want to lie their way into a war was beyond me.

"Where's your brother?" I asked Little John.

"Dead," he said, and he started sniffling again. "He got himself killed at Bull Run. Lots of my buddies are dead."

Joshua lowered Rufus and Alexander into the graves he had dug. Mom and I covered them with dirt. Little John made a homemade tombstone out of a piece of wood. He stuck it into the dirt and cried some more. Willie couldn't do much because of his arm, but he said a prayer over the graves. We took off our hats and lowered our heads.

"They were good men," Joshua said sadly. "Coulda been any of us."

"Could be any of us tomorrow," Little John said solemnly.

"I reckon if a bullet ain't found me yet, it ain't gonna find me," said Joshua.

"That's what I thought yesterday," Willie said. "But a bullet found me today, and I didn't like it none."

Rufus had obviously been shot, but Alexander didn't have any blood on him. I asked Little John what he died from.

"Diarrhea," he said.

"Diarrhea?"

I thought it was a joke, at first. I mean, diarrhea is *funny*. But Little John wasn't laughing, and neither was anybody else. Mom leaned over and whispered to me that in this time, soldiers were just as likely to die from diarrhea or some other disease as they were from a bullet. They simply didn't have the medicine to cure things.

I fussed with my uniform. I was wearing the clothes of a guy who had died from diarrhea. I didn't feel too good about it. My hand brushed against one of Alexander's pockets, and it felt like something was in there. I reached inside and pulled out a sheet of paper. The others wanted to know what it said, so I unfolded it and read it to them . . .

> *Dearest Molly,*
> *Sorry I don't write oftener. I pray these words reach you by August, when my 2 years in the army will be done and I can return home so we might be wed. We*

are marching to Gettysburg today, and the boys say we will meet General Lee's army there. In the event that I fall, dear Molly, this letter shall serve as a reminder that my love for you is forever. I will never forget the blissful moments we spent together. My only regret will be not seeing the children we would have raised together. When my last breath escapes me it will whisper your name, Molly. If the dead can return to this earth, I will surely return to your side and be with you always. When you feel a breeze brush your cheek, it shall be me, whispering that I love you.

Yours,
Alexander

I folded up the letter and handed it to Willie, who said he would make sure Molly got it.

It was quiet for a while. Finally Little John broke the silence and asked, "You think Rufus and Alexander are cold down there?"

"They don't feel nothin'," Willie said. "They're dead."

That seemed to be the signal that the funeral was over. Little John gathered up some wood and Joshua built a small fire. They unrolled their sleeping blankets, where they had stored some of their food.

"Willie was bleedin' pretty bad, ma'am," Joshua

said to Mom. "You might of saved his life."

"I was just doing my job," Mom replied.

"I'm obliged all the same," Willie said.

"It would sure please us if you and your boy, Stosh, would join us for vittles this evening," said Joshua. "It's the least we can do to say thanks."

"We got two extra rations," Willie said, glancing at the graves.

Oh great. Now I would have to eat a dead guy's *food*.

I was hungry, but the stuff they were taking out of their blankets didn't look very appetizing. I would much rather have eaten at home. And as exciting as the battle had been, I didn't exactly want to stick around to see another one. One of those bullets could very easily find me or my mom. I didn't want either one of us to end up like Rufus or Alexander.

"Let's go," I whispered to Mom.

She shot me the look that meant I didn't say the polite thing.

"We would be delighted to join you gentlemen for . . . vittles," Mom said.

"Great," Willie said. "Got any eatables?"

"It just so happens that I do." Mom opened up her purse and put all her goodies on the blanket that Little John had spread out on the ground. Juice boxes. Peanut butter crackers. Go-Gurt.

The three of them stopped what they were doing and stared at Mom's snacks.

"What the devil is that?" Joshua finally asked.

"Go-Gurt," I said, ripping open the tube, "Portable yogurt."

"What's yogurt?" Little John asked.

I looked at Mom. Mom looked at me. I must have eaten a million gallons of yogurt in my life, and I had to admit I had no idea what the stuff was. Something to do with milk, I think.

"You'll like these peanut butter crackers," I said, changing the subject.

"Butter made from goobers?" Willie asked, wrinkling up his nose. "I think not."

"Have you got any hot dogs?" I asked. They all looked at me strangely, and instantly I realized that hot dogs did not exist back then.

"You eat . . . *dog*?" Little John asked.

"How about a juice box?" Mom asked. She stuck the straw in the box and offered it to Joshua.

"You put juice . . . in a . . . box?" he said, examining it.

"Where'd you say you was from?" Willie asked.

"Louisville, Kentucky," I said.

"Oh," Willie said, as if that explained everything.

"I hear tell Kentucky folks do some strange things," Joshua said, and he took a sip from the straw. A smile broke across his face, and he said it was the finest apple juice he had ever tasted. Mom passed around a few juice boxes.

"How do you fit the dang apple in the box?" Little John asked.

I couldn't answer that one either. But it didn't

matter. We had a fine picnic. Joshua stuck something he called "salt beef" on to the end of his bayonet and held it over the fire to roast it. It was hard to chew, but okay. Willie and Little John contributed beans, rice, and some crackers they called "hardtack." That stuff tasted like chalk. They topped off the feast with some cherries, which they had picked in the fields while they were marching to Gettysburg. Sometimes, they said, they got corn bread, dried potatoes, or turnips.

I wasn't entirely comfortable sitting there eating. What would happen if the Confederates decided to suddenly come back and launch a surprise attack? They could wipe out the whole Union army while we were having dinner. I kept standing up and peering over the ridge to be sure nobody was coming.

"Sit yourself down," Joshua said. "The Rebs skedaddled, and they're lickin' their wounds. They'd be crazy to attack us on this hill now."

"Rebs *are* crazy," Willie said.

"They ain't *that* crazy," said Joshua. "And they're hungry too, just like us."

"I heard the Rebs cut off folks' ears, and they boil babies for breakfast," Little John volunteered.

"Oh, that's just talk," Joshua said.

It occurred to me that these guys had no radio and no TV. There were no movies, no Internet. Some of them probably never even went to school. They only knew what they experienced personally or read in the newspapers, if they could even read at all. Everything else was just rumor.

"I heard the Rebs are gonna try to kill President Lincoln," Joshua said as he bit off a piece of salt beef.

"They try that, and I'll kill every last one of 'em myself," Willie said, "even with this bum arm."

I was about to tell them that I knew Lincoln would be assassinated, but Mom glanced over at me and shook her head no. She was probably right. It might not be such a hot idea to let anybody know we were from the twenty-first century.

Joshua heated up a pot of coffee over the fire. I never liked the taste of coffee, but the others were drinking it, so I had a cup.

Mom had been pretty quiet, eating and listening to the soldiers talk. She only interrupted a few times to say how tasty the beef was or to ask for a chunk of hardtack.

"I would be very curious to know if you fellows support this war," she said, almost out of the blue.

"Mom!"

"What?"

"You're trying to make this"—and I said the last word under my breath—"educational!"

"I am not!" she insisted. "I simply want to understand why these boys are willing to risk their lives. Why are you fighting this Civil War?"

I rolled my eyes. What a liar she is. I should have known it would only be a matter of time before she tried to turn this whole thing into a history lesson. That's just the way she is.

"Civil War?" Joshua spit into the fire. "Ain't nothing civil about it."

"I'll tell you what I'm fighting for," Willie said. "Thirteen dollars a month. That, and for the chance to kill as many Johnnies as I can."

"Fightin' beats workin' on my pa's farm," Little John said. "There I had nothin'. Here I got three square meals a day, a paycheck, and when I come home the girls will treat me like a hero."

"Maybe a dead hero," Joshua said.

"But I thought the war was about slavery," Mom said. I rolled my eyes. If she'd had a blackboard with her, she would be writing a lesson plan on it.

"I don't care a lick about slavery," Little John said. "I never even met a Negro in my life."

"I never met a *Southerner* in my life," Willie said. "Heck, none of us ain't ever even been outside of Pennsylvania."

"The Declaration of Independence said all men are created equal," Joshua said. "That's what Mr. Thomas Jefferson said, and he was a lot smarter than the Rebs."

"Jefferson kept slaves," Little John said. "So did Washington. They all did."

"If all men are created equal," Willie asked, "how come there ain't no rich boys out here fightin'? 'Cause it's a rich man's war and a poor boy's fight. That's why."

"Don't say nothin' in the Constitution about slavery," Little John said.

"How would you know, Little John?" Joshua laughed. "You can't read."

"Well, I had it read *to* me," Little John said. "And it don't mention slaves nowhere."

"Look," Joshua said, "it boils down to this. Slavery or liberty. It's one or the other. That's why it's called the *United* States. A country can't have both. We're fightin' to save the Union."

"Well, which is it?" Little John asked. "The Union or the slaves? We better be riskin' our necks for somethin' worthwhile, that's all I got to say."

Little John looked over at the graves. I thought he might cry again.

"I'm fightin' to save my own neck," Willie said. "If I kill a Reb and he don't kill me, I done good. That's all I know."

"Well, I think they shoulda took care of the problem back in 1776," Little John said. "If they didn't want slavery, they shoulda got rid of it then."

"Well, they didn't," Joshua said. "So *we* got to."

Off in the distance there was a loud boom. We all turned our heads in the direction of the sound.

"That's a thirty-pounder," Joshua said. "It can fire a shell more'n two miles. The Rebs ain't quittin'."

"Reckon it's easier for folks to fight it out than it is to figure it out," Joshua said, ending the discussion.

Suddenly I realized how tired I was. It really was time to be getting back home. Joshua and Willie and Little John started cleaning up from dinner. Mom and I helped. There was another cannon blast in the distance.

"We been fightin' this thing out for two years," Willie said. "Maybe we'll just fight it out forever."

"I think it's almost over," Joshua said. "I got a sense."

"You think we're gonna lose this war?" Little John asked, almost fearfully.

"Well, here's the way I see it," Joshua said, spitting into the fire. "We lose here at Gettysburg and the war might be over. The Rebs can just march to Washington and take the city. That'll be the end of the United States. Eighty years. They'll say democracy didn't work. But if we *win* here, the war might be over too. The Rebs won't have no army left. That's why I think it's almost over, one way or another."

"We ain't gonna lose," Willie insisted.

"They got General Robert E. Lee on their side," Little John said.

"So what?" Joshua said. "We got General Meade. He's a good man too."

"Yeah, but Meade is the third general we had this year," Little John said, "He only took command a few days ago."

"And Doubleday ain't got no idea what he's doin'," said Willie.

My ears perked up.

"Wait a minute," I said. "Did you say Doubleday?"

"Sure," Willie said. "General Doubleday."

"Would that be General *Abner* Doubleday?"

"Well, of course that would be General Abner Doubleday. Don't know of no other General Doubleday."

Suddenly I wasn't tired anymore.

10

Dirty Work

SO IT WASN'T ALL A BIG TIME TRAVEL MIX-UP! ABNER Doubleday *was* here! He was a general in the Union army. That's why Mom and I ended up at Gettysburg.

"General Doubleday took command of First Corps just this morning," Joshua told me, "after General Reynolds was killed."

According to Joshua, General Reynolds was sitting on his horse near McPherson's Ridge when a Confederate sharpshooter hiding in the woods picked him off. The bullet went in one side of his head and came out the other. He died instantly. He was replaced by his second in command, General Abner Doubleday.

"And he's the guy who invented baseball, right?" I asked.

"Don't know nothin' about that," Joshua said.

Willie and Little John looked at me like I was crazy. For all I knew, they had never even heard of baseball.

"Can you take me to General Doubleday?" I asked excitedly. "I've got to ask him a very important question."

"Me, I got things to do," Joshua said. "Got to fortify this position tonight. Bobby Lee and the Rebs are sure to come back at us with all they got at first light tomorrow morning."

"I'll take 'em to Doubleday," Willie said. "I ain't much good with this bum arm anyhow."

"Okay," Joshua said, "But I need Little John."

I said good-bye, and Willie led my mom and me on a search for Abner Doubleday. It wasn't going to be easy, Willie warned me. There were about eighty thousand Union soldiers at Gettysburg. Most of them were at Cemetery Ridge and Culp's Hill. But the battlefield covered six square miles, and the first day of fighting had scattered soldiers everywhere. We might never find Doubleday. He might have been killed too.

Still, it was worth it to try. I hadn't traveled a century and a half just to give up now.

We were no more than fifty yards from the ditch when I was hit by a sight that I will never forget.

Death. Everywhere.

Bodies were scattered across the field so thickly that you could barely walk without stepping on them. Blue uniforms and gray ones. Dead horses lying on their side. Puddles of blood in the grass, and streaks of it on rocks and trees. Flies buzzing around bodies and buzzards circling overhead. Ten yards from a body we would see an arm or a leg that once belonged to it. It was disgusting.

The sun was getting lower in the sky, but it was still hot. The smell of blood, sweat, and skunk hung in the air. I couldn't blame a skunk for spraying. Willie gave Mom and me handkerchiefs to hold over our noses.

"Watch out for sharpshooters," Willie advised us as we walked around one of the craters that dotted the battlefield. "They mostly aim for officers, but you never know." I scanned the distant woods to see if anyone was hiding up in the trees.

Soldiers were going from corpse to corpse, removing weapons, ammunition, canteens, blankets, and supplies. Anything that might be useful. The dead would not be needing any of it.

Another group of soldiers was picking up bodies and carrying them off the battlefield to be sent home to their families. If a body couldn't be identified, it was buried right where the man had fallen. In some cases, bodies were being stacked in mass graves.

It occurred to me that all these men had died right next to a cemetery. It seemed kind of . . . convenient.

I was surprised to see some Confederate soldiers out there on the field picking up their dead right alongside the Union soldiers. It was so *weird*. Half an hour ago the soldiers on both sides had been trying their best to kill each other. Now they were chatting with each other as they did their morbid work, sometimes stopping to swap food, tobacco, or news with the other side.

It kind of made sense, in a way. They were all Americans. They spoke the same language. Most of them had the same religion, the same heroes, the same history. Some of them came from the same families. What was harder to understand was why these Americans were fighting each other in the first place.

"Anybody see General Doubleday?" we asked as we stepped gingerly around the bodies. Nobody seemed to know where he could be found.

One guy said he thought he saw Doubleday back behind Cemetery Ridge, so we circled away from the battlefield and up the hill. Union soldiers were building barricades at the top of the hill out of stone and logs to defend against tomorrow's Rebel charge. We asked if they had seen Doubleday, but they just shook their heads.

There was a sign at the gate of the cemetery that read: "All persons found using firearms in these grounds will be prosecuted with the utmost vigor of"—I couldn't read the rest of the words. They were filled with bullet holes.

In the cemetery itself, some soldiers were sitting against tombstones, asleep. Or maybe they were dead. It was hard to tell. Every so often I'd see someone just sitting there sobbing over a grave he had dug. We didn't bother those people with questions.

Behind the Union line, it was like a small city. There were little white tents as far as you could see, and just about as many campfires. Soldiers were everywhere, and everybody looked busy. They were cooking and eating their dinner. Some were cleaning their guns, chopping wood, or grooming their horses. Guys sat against trees, writing letters or reading letters from home. Some were shaving or brushing their teeth. Some played checkers, cards, or dominos. It all looked very . . . normal.

"Seen Doubleday?" we asked everyone.

Rumors were flying around. I heard a soldier say the Union had lost ten thousand men today, and the Rebels as nearly as many. The 24th Michigan regiment supposedly lost five hundred out of its six hundred men.

We passed by a big tent filled with guys playing with some little machines and listening intently while they scribbled in notebooks. I realized they were telegraph operators, sending home news about the war. These guys must be the nineteenth-century equivalent to computer geeks, it occurred to me. They didn't know where Doubleday was either.

A soldier limped by with a cannonball chained to his leg. I asked Willie about it, and he said the guy was probably caught sitting down on guard duty. Another guy had a big letter C branded into his forehead.

"Coward," Willie explained.

"Have you seen General Doubleday?" I asked a man rushing by us.

"No, and I don't reckon to," he replied. "I'm going home."

"If they catch you, you could be shot for desertion," Willie warned the guy.

"If I stay, I could be shot by Rebs," the guy said, and he continued on his way.

I was starting to get frustrated. Why did this happen every time I traveled through time? I would always wind up somewhere *near* the person I was trying to meet, but not right next to him.

Willie Biddle looked like he was running out of patience, and so was Mom. She'd never had much interest in finding Abner Doubleday in the first place. As we walked around the Union camp, she became increasingly concerned with the dirt and filth the soldiers were living in.

"Look at this!" Mom said, aghast. "The latrine runs right into the source of their drinking water. No wonder men are dying of dysentery and diarrhea. I can only imagine the medical facilities around here. Where are the ambulances?"

"Mom," I whispered, so Willie wouldn't hear, "this is 1863. They didn't have ambulances."

"There's an ambulance right over there, ma'am," Willie said.

The "ambulance" was a large wooden wagon pulled by horses. There were six or seven ragged-looking Union soldiers in it. Some of them were moaning, and others were crying out for their wives, their girlfriends, or their mothers. One of them just sat there silently, like he was in shock. They all had a look of fear in their eyes.

"Food, please," one of the wounded men begged the driver. "I haven't eaten in two days."

"Rations go first to those men who are fit for fightin'," said the driver. "Orders from General Meade."

Mom walked right up to the driver.

"I'm a nurse," she said. "Can you take us to the hospital?"

"Ma'am, that's directly where I'm goin'," he said. "Hop on."

"Not the *hospital*!" moaned one of the injured soldiers. "I don't want to go! Let me die here."

"You'll be fine," my mother assured him, and she climbed up next to the driver.

"Mom, I want to find Abner Doubleday," I complained.

"Doubleday can wait," she replied. "There are men dying here."

"I'm getting out of here," said Willie. "Doctors scare me."

I said good-bye to Willie Biddle and climbed up next to Mom. It didn't take long to get to the hospital, but the road was unpaved and the ride was bumpy. Every time the wheels hit a rut, the soldiers in the back cried out in pain. I felt sorry for them.

The driver stopped the wagon outside a big tent. I only knew it was the hospital because there were a bunch of soldiers lying on the ground outside, moaning and screaming in pain. Some of them looked like they were in really bad shape.

"Dreadful conditions," Mom said as we climbed off the wagon.

"I need some help in here!" somebody shouted from inside the tent.

"Mom, don't!" I said, holding her back. "It's not your job."

"Yes it is."

"Well, I'll wait out here," I said. "There's too much blood around here, and a lot of it is on the outside of people instead of inside, where it belongs."

"I want you to come with me," Mom said, pulling me into the tent. "If we get separated, we may never find each other again."

It was horrible in there. It looked horrible, it sounded horrible, and it smelled horrible.

There were no beds or curtains or flowers in this hospital. A wounded soldier was lying across a big plank of wood that was supported by two wooden crates. That was the operating table. The plank was covered with a rubber sheet. Underneath the table was a tub splattered with blood that had dripped down from the plank.

The doctor was sweating. His sleeves were rolled up, and his white shirt and apron were soaked with blood. There was a wooden box next to him filled with weird-looking medical instruments.

"I've been working for six straight hours," he said wearily. "I could use a hand."

"I'll do whatever I can to help, Doctor," Mom said.

Mom must have been freaking out. At the hospital where she works, they've got all kinds of high-tech stuff. MRI machines. Lasers that do all kinds of surgery. Hemostatic bandages. This hospital probably didn't even have X rays or antibiotics. This doctor had probably never even heard of germs or aspirin. On a table next to the operating table there were bottles filled with stuff like "dandelion root." A lot of good *that* would do. But it was the only medicine they had.

"That's a nasty wound you've got there," the doctor told the injured man after a short examination. "I'm going to have to take that leg off."

"No!" the guy screamed. "Not my leg!"

"Is that really necessary, Doctor?" Mom asked.

"Of course it's necessary," he replied. "If the leg gets infected, this man will die."

I turned my head away. No way I was going to watch him chop off the guy's leg. But when I looked in the corner of the tent, there was an even more repulsive sight. There was a huge pile of arms and legs that had already been chopped off. They were just sitting there. Some of the legs still had shoes on them. Flies were buzzing around them. I felt like I might throw up.

The doctor picked up this big saw and sloshed it around in a pan of dirty water for a few seconds. Then he wiped it on his apron, which was already red with blood.

"Aren't you going to sterilize that, Doctor?" Mom asked, alarmed. "He'll get gangrene!"

"Don't be ridiculous," the doctor replied. "Gangrene is caused by bad air. Didn't they teach you that in nursing school?"

The poor guy on the table was screaming and whining and praying and begging to be left alone all at the same time.

"You're lucky they hit you in the leg," the doctor told the guy. "If they'd got you in the gut, there would be nothing I could do."

"I don't wanna die!" screamed the guy on the table.

"Hold him down!" instructed the doctor. "You're not going to die, son."

I grabbed the soldier's arms to prevent him from thrashing around.

"Don't you have any anesthesia?" Mom asked desperately. "Chloroform? Ether? Nitrous oxide?"

"We ran out weeks ago," the doctor replied, "and Mr. Lincoln hasn't sent us more yet."

"Even opium or morphine would help him bear the pain," Mom said hopefully.

"Give him some of this," the doctor said, taking a thin metal flask out of his pocket and handing it to Mom. She poured something into the guy's mouth. I could smell the alcohol. Then the doctor took a bullet out of his other pocket.

"This is going to pinch a little," he told the soldier as he put the bullet between the man's teeth. "It won't hurt so much if you bite on the bullet."

I didn't watch, but I couldn't block out the horrible sounds—the screaming, the saw cutting through the leg, the thud when the leg hit the ground. The doctor tossed it on the pile with the others.

"No! No! Nooooooooo!" the poor guy screamed. Mom held his hand.

The doctor sloshed the saw in the dirty water again and took a deep breath.

"Next!" he called, as he wiped the sweat off his forehead. Two guys came in, put the poor guy on a stretcher, and carried him out.

"Aren't you going to sew up the wound?" Mom asked.

"I'm a surgeon, ma'am," the doctor said. "They can patch him up outside. Next!"

Another injured guy was carried in on a stretcher and put onto the bloody table. He was soaking wet, and his shirt was pulled over his face. His arms were flailing around like he was a crazy man. He was shorter than the guy whose leg was amputated.

"I don't know if this one's gonna make it, Doc," said one of the guys carrying the stretcher. "He ain't breathing. We found him in the pond. Smacked his head good too."

The doctor pulled the shirt down off the soldier's

face, and it took me a second or two to realize that the face looked familiar.

"Little John!" I hollered.

Little John didn't recognize me. He didn't recognize anything. His eyes were closed.

"Another drunk," mumbled the doctor.

"He's not a drunk!" I shouted. "He's my friend! You've got to save him! Mom, you've got to *do* something!"

"I'm going to do a bleeding," the doctor said. "Nurse, will you hand me the hot iron, please?"

"This boy has lost a lot of blood already!" Mom said. "Why would you want him to bleed further?"

"Bleeding cleanses the system," the doctor said, as if that explained anything. "It will save his life."

"If his blood pressure drops too far, he'll go into shock!" Mom said, raising her voice a little.

The doctor stopped what he was doing and looked at Mom.

"Excuse me, ma'am, but are you a doctor?"

"No, but—"

"Then kindly keep your opinions to yourself!"

On the table, Little John had stopped thrashing his arms around. He was lying there quietly now. Too quietly. It didn't look like he was breathing.

"*Now* look what you've done!" the doctor scolded Mom. "This boy is dead. Next!"

"Wait a minute!" Mom shouted, elbowing the doctor out of the way.

Mom leaned over Little John. She tilted his head

back and put her ear to his mouth to listen for breathing. After a few seconds she pinched his nostrils closed with two fingers and opened his mouth with her other hand. Then she put her mouth, open wide, right on top of Little John's lips.

"Are you insane, woman?" the doctor hollered. "Stop kissing that boy! Have you no respect for the dead?"

He tried to push Mom out of the way, but I gave him a shove that sent him falling into the pile of amputated arms and legs.

Mom blew some air into Little John's mouth, and then took her mouth away. She took a deep breath and did it again. Little John's chest went up, but it didn't look like he was conscious. Mom blew air into his mouth a few more times and checked for a pulse on his neck.

"Is he dead, Mom?"

"I'm not sure," she said.

Mom climbed up on top of the table and straddled over Little John, with one knee on either side of him. She put her hands together against his chest and began pushing down on it, over and over again.

"Get off that man!" the doctor said, struggling to his feet. "He's dead! You're a sick, perverted woman!"

"Nobody calls my mother a pervert!" I yelled, and I socked the doctor right in the face. I got him good too, and he landed in the pile of limbs again.

Mom kept pumping on Little John's chest.

Suddenly he coughed violently, shook his head, and opened his eyes.

"Little John!" I shouted. Mom climbed down from the table.

"Stosh! What are you doing here?"

"We were looking for Abner Doubleday," I told him. "What happened to you?"

"Joshua told me to fetch some water, and I fell into the pond," he said, sitting up on the table. "Can't swim."

By that time, the doctor had struggled to his feet again. He was rubbing his jaw.

"It's a miracle!" he said, looking at Little John.

"It's CPR," Mom replied matter-of-factly. "Look, if you've got a patient who isn't breathing, don't worry about his blood or his wound. He's going to suffocate before he bleeds to death. You've got to make sure he has an open airway and get some air into his lungs. If that doesn't work, pump his chest until he comes to. Understand?"

"Uh . . . yes, ma'am," the doctor said.

"Sorry I punched you," I told the doctor.

Mom and I helped Little John off the table, and we walked him out of the tent. Mom's nurse's uniform, which was caked with mud when we walked in there, was now splotched with blood.

Outside, a bunch of soldiers stared at Mom and stepped out of her way like she was somebody famous. They must have been listening to what was going on inside the tent.

"Wow, Mom, you're a hero!" I said.

"Oh, stop it," she replied. "We do this every day at the hospital."

We weren't more than a few feet outside the tent when a guy on a horse galloped over. He stopped the horse right in front of us.

"Atten-tion!" somebody hollered, and all the soldiers stood up straight and saluted the guy on the horse. I figured he must be a major or somebody really important.

"Good evening, General Doubleday," one of the soldiers said.

11

Poppycock and Flapdoodle

IT WAS *HIM*! I COULDN'T BELIEVE IT. AFTER ALL MOM AND I had been through, we had finally found the one and only Abner Doubleday, the man who invented baseball.

Or the man who *might have* invented baseball, anyway. That was what I was about to find out. I felt my pocket to make sure the baseball was still there.

"At ease, men."

Doubleday saluted the soldiers as he hopped down off the horse. He looked pretty much the way he did in the photo. He was almost six feet tall, maybe forty years old or so. His uniform looked cleaner and less wrinkled than everyone else's. Generals, I guess, didn't have to do the dirty work of fighting.

He walked right up to Mom, removed his hat, and bowed before her. His bushy hair fell mostly over one side of his head.

"Is this the nurse of whom I've heard?" Doubleday asked. "I wished to meet the lady personally and issue my sincerest gratitude for the service she has rendered to our noble cause."

"That'd be her, sir," Little John said. "If not for her, I'd be dead and buried, sir. She saved my buddy Willie Biddle up on Cemetery Ridge too."

"Is this true, ma'am?"

"It was really nothing," Mom said, embarrassed. "Anybody could have done it."

"What is your name, ma'am?"

"Terry Stoshack, sir," Mom said, shaking Doubleday's hand, "and this is my son, Joey."

"That is an unusual nurse's uniform you are wearing, Mrs. Stoshack," Doubleday said. "What regiment are you with?"

"Uh . . . regiment? Well . . ."

"They're with the 151st Pennsylvania, sir," volunteered Little John.

"Ma'am," Doubleday said, "because of your courage and skill in the face of this horrific battle, I am going to recommend that President Lincoln award you the Medal of Honor."

The soldiers gasped. Mom blushed. I was truly proud of her.

"Thank you, sir!" Mom said. She wasn't sure if she was supposed to salute or curtsy, so she did both.

Finally, it was my chance. I didn't know if

Doubleday was going to hang around some more telling Mom how great she was, or if he was about to turn on his heel to go congratulate somebody else for an act of bravery.

"General Doubleday," I said, stepping up to the man. "May I ask you a question, sir?"

"Certainly, young fellow. What is it?"

I took a deep breath to collect my thoughts.

"Sir, did you invent baseball?"

Abner Doubleday stopped and peered at me for a few seconds. Instantly I regretted asking the question. Thousands of American soldiers had been killed on this horrible day. He had come over to thank Mom for saving lives. And here I was, asking him about something silly like baseball. I was afraid he was going to snap my head off.

"Invent *what*?" he finally asked.

A crazy thought crossed my mind. What if Doubleday didn't invent baseball? And what if baseball didn't even exist in 1863? I would look *really* stupid.

"B-baseball," I stuttered, taking the ball out of my pocket. "The game of baseball. You know, bats, balls, gloves . . ."

"Young man, are you insane?" Doubleday thundered. "Who told you I invented the game of baseball?"

"This guy named Flip Valentini," I said. "He's my Little League coach, and he's a really cool guy, and he said—"

Mom stopped me before I could say anything even stupider.

"Poppycock!" the general said, climbing back on his horse. "Me, invent baseball? That's balderdash! Blather! Twaddle! Flapdoodle!"

I didn't know what any of those words meant, but I kind of had the feeling the answer to my question was no.

I was a little disappointed, I must admit. It would have been cool to meet the guy who invented baseball. Mom and I had been through a lot to meet Doubleday, and I was rooting for him to be the guy. I went to put the baseball back in my pocket.

"What's that?" Doubleday asked.

"A baseball," I said. "I was going to ask you to sign it. But if you didn't invent baseball, it probably doesn't matter."

Mom grabbed the ball and held it out to Doubleday.

"I would consider it a personal favor, sir, if you could put your autograph on this ball for my son," Mom said. She pulled the Sharpie out of her purse. Doubleday looked at the Sharpie curiously.

"Where does one insert the ink?" he asked.

"The ink is already in there," I said. "You just press on the tip."

Doubleday shook his head and examined the Sharpie again. Then he wrote his name on the ball and handed it to me.

"Pennsylvania, eh?" he said, looking at me and

Mom curiously. "I was not aware of such odd customs and implements here in Pennsylvania."

With that, he galloped away.

"Are you happy now?" Mom asked. "You got the answer to your question, and you got a souvenir too."

"I'm happy, Mom," I said, throwing an arm around her. "Let's go home."

We said good-bye to Little John, and Mom told him to be careful not to fall into any more ponds, because she wouldn't be around to rescue him next time.

We had to find a quiet place to sit down. When I travel through time, I need to focus my concentration as strongly as I can. There was a clump of trees about a hundred yards behind us. That looked like a good place.

I didn't know what time it was. The sun was dipping lower in the sky, and a full moon was starting to become visible, but there was still some daylight. It was summer, I remembered, and it stayed light until nine o'clock or even later.

As we walked over to the woods, Mom pulled out the pack of baseball cards we had brought with us and handed it to me. One of those cards would be our ticket home.

"What's that sound, Joey?" Mom asked, taking my hand as we walked among the trees.

I could see a clearing past the woods. It sounded like there might be people out there. It was more than that. I heard a sharp crack too, like a rock hitting a tree or something. It was an oddly familiar sound.

As we came through the trees into a big open field, I realized that the sound I heard was the sound of a bat hitting a ball.

They were playing baseball out there!

12

Rules Are Rules

"COME ON, SHOW SOME GINGER!" A TALL GUY WITH RED hair hollered as he tossed a ball up in the air and fungoed a pop fly to the players scattered around the field.

They had created a homemade baseball diamond by placing four pieces of wood around the field where the bases should be. There were no dugouts, foul lines, or fences, of course. It was all very improvised, like a pickup game back home. Mom and I sat down on the grass to watch.

The tall guy wasn't holding a regular baseball bat. He was swinging the wooden spoke of a wagon wheel that had busted apart. The wagon was lying on its side near a tree.

He wasn't hitting a ball, either. It looked like a rolled-up sock with a rock inside it or something. It was pretty pathetic.

The fielders didn't have any gloves. They were catching the ball bare-handed. Some of them were still wearing their army uniforms. Others had stripped them off and were playing in their underwear.

The thing that struck me most was how *happy* they all seemed. It was like they had forgotten all about the horrible battle they had fought just hours earlier. I guess everybody copes with stressful situations in different ways. Some people sit down next to a gravestone and cry. Some go into shock. And some play a game.

I was anxious to get back home to Louisville, but it felt so good sitting out there on the grass. The sun was going down, and it wasn't so hot anymore. A breeze was blowing through the trees. Mom and I decided to watch for a few minutes before going home.

It was nice to be away from the war. I could imagine how much nicer it was for the soldiers. Some of them had been fighting for two years.

They probably saw Mom and me sitting there watching them, but they didn't pay us any mind. Mom massaged the back of my neck with her fingers as we watched them, the way she used to do when I was little.

The tall guy was pretty good with the bat, but then he fouled one off deep into the woods. After some good-natured cursing, the players went to look for the ball. A few minutes later they straggled back out of the woods. Nobody had found it.

"Sorry, gents," the tall guy said. "Looks like we've got to call it a day."

I felt the baseball in my pocket that Abner Doubleday had signed. Some of these guys had probably never even *seen* a real baseball, it occurred to me.

"You think I should let them use it?" I asked Mom.

"It's up to you, Joey. It's your ball."

I thought it over. The baseball *did* look pretty new for a Civil War ball. It could use some dirt marks. That would make it look more real.

"Hey!" I shouted, "I've got a baseball!"

"Toss it here," one of the players said. I whipped the ball to him, and he caught it on a fly.

"By thunder, that's some arm you got on you, son!" he said as he examined the ball. "Care to join us?"

"Can I play, Mom?" I pleaded. "Just for a few minutes?"

"Sure, Joey," she said, mussing up my hair. "Have fun. We'll go home whenever you're ready."

I ran off to join the players. The tall guy seemed to be running things. He told me to grab the bat and take a turn at the plate.

Well, actually, he didn't say that at all. What he said was, "Striker to the line. What's your name, son? Step up to the home base."

"Joe Stoshack," I said. "But people call me Stosh."

"Then that's what we'll call you," he said. "My

name is Charles Chadwick, but most people call me Monkeywrench."

Monkeywrench went out to the mound, which wasn't a mound at all but just the spot where the mound would be if they had one. He said he needed to take a few warm-up pitches.

I picked up the bat and swung it around a few times. It was way too long and heavy for me. It was way too long and heavy for *anybody*. I noticed the first, second, and third basemen were playing right on their bases. It was like it hadn't occurred to them that they could cover more fair territory if they played away from the base.

Monkeywrench didn't go into a regular pitcher's windup. He took a running start and whipped the ball underhand. The catcher didn't squat right behind the plate. He stood about ten feet back. I didn't blame him. Without a chest protector, mask, or glove, I wouldn't want to be right behind the batter either. One of the other players took position behind the catcher to call balls and strikes.

"Whatcher pleasure, son?" the umpire asked me.

"I beg your pardon?"

"High or low?" said the ump.

"Huh?"

"Ya wanna high pitch or a low pitch?" he said slowly, as if I was stupid.

"I get to *choose*?" I asked.

"Lordy! Of course ya get to choose," said the ump. "Ain'tcha never played baseball before?"

"High," I said sheepishly. I've always been a high ball hitter.

"Very well then."

Monkeywrench rubbed the ball in his hands and started swinging his arms around. Then he took a running start and whipped the ball toward me. It was up around my eyes, so I let it go.

"Fair!" called the ump.

"What do you mean, fair?" I asked.

"It was a fair pitch," he replied. "Strike one."

I wasn't about to argue. I choked up on the bat and took my stance.

"Strike it hard, Stosh!" one of the players hollered.

The next pitch bounced in the dirt in front of the plate. The umpire called it "unfair." One and one.

I looked over a second strike which was, in my opinion, way outside. One and two. Now I had to protect the plate.

"Well done, sir!" somebody hollered at Monkeywrench.

The next pitch was way inside. I jumped out of the way, but the ball glanced off my leg. I tossed the bat aside and trotted to first base.

"Where do you think you're going?" asked the ump.

"I got hit by the pitch," I said. "Duh!"

"So what?" the ump said. "Get back in there and take your licks. The count is two balls and two strikes."

Sheesh, this was going to take some getting used to. Their dumb rules were starting to make me mad.

"Come on," I yelled to Monkeywrench, "get it over!"

The next pitch looked good enough, so I took a poke at it and hit a grounder toward second base.

"Huzzah! Well struck!" somebody yelled as I dug for first. "Leg it, son!"

I was a stride or two from the base when the ball hit me right between the shoulder blades.

"Owwww!" I moaned as I crossed the bag. Either that second baseman had really bad aim, or he threw the ball at me on purpose. Well, at least I was safe.

"You're out!" the ump said.

"What do you mean I'm out?" I complained. "The ball hit me!"

"That's why you're out," said the second baseman.

"Did you do that on *purpose*?" I asked him.

"Sure I did," he said.

"Why didn't you throw the ball to the first baseman?"

"Why should I?" he asked. "It was easier to soak you."

"Soak me?"

I tried to rub the spot on my back where the ball had hit me, but I couldn't reach it. There would be a big bruise there the next day, I could tell. I looked over to where my mother was sitting and watching. She just shrugged.

Monkeywrench could tell I was upset, and he told the others that seeing as how I didn't know the rules of the game very well, he was going to give me another turn at bat.

This time I was determined not to let the pitcher or the second baseman or anybody else hit me with the ball. I gripped the bat tightly and took a cut at the first pitch, even though it was out of my strike zone. I hit it pretty well, a clean single to right field. The ball bounced once on the grass, and the outfielder threw it in. I pulled up to first base and threw a thumbs-up sign to my mother.

"You're out!" the umpire yelled.

"What do you mean, I'm out!" I hollered. "That was a single!"

"The fielder caught the ball on the first bounce," the umpire said. "So you're out."

"What?!"

Now I was *really* mad. These people were a bunch of morons! They had no idea how to play baseball. Catching the ball on a bounce was an *out*? You get hit by a pitch and you don't get to go to first, but the fielders can hit you with the ball to put you out? I was stomping around, yelling and complaining.

Monkeywrench came over to me and told me to calm down. "Perhaps you would be better as a hurler," he suggested. "I know you got a good arm on you."

"Well, okay," I said, trying to control myself.

He handed me the ball. I was just about to take a warm-up pitch when suddenly everybody on the field stood up straight and saluted.

"Atten-tion!"

A guy in a blue uniform came out of the woods, and I could tell right away it was Abner Doubleday. He wasn't on his horse anymore.

I figured that Doubleday was going to break up the game and tell the players to go back to their posts, or something like that. But he didn't. He just mumbled, "At ease," and sat down heavily on a tree stump near home plate.

"I have been relieved of my command," he said gloomily.

"Why, sir?" Monkeywrench asked. Some of the players gathered around Doubleday.

"The Confederates broke through my line for a brief time today," he said, resting his head in his hands. "My men were forced to retreat. General Meade believes my men acted with cowardice. I am to report to Washington to explain my actions."

He looked so sad, sitting there on the tree stump. I thought he was about to cry or something. I wished there was something I could do to make him feel better.

"Say, General!" called out one of the players. "Perhaps you would like to take a turn as striker?"

"No thank you," Doubleday said. "I do not much cotton to the physical exertions."

"Might perk up your spirits, sir," said Monkeywrench.

"Never played the game," he said.

"Never too late to start, sir," one player said.

"There's always a first time for everything, sir," added another.

"Well, I suppose there would be no harm," Doubleday said, getting up from the stump.

I shot a look over at Mom. I was going to be pitching to Abner Doubleday! Even if he *didn't* invent baseball, this was going to be cool.

"High or low, sir?" asked the ump.

"High, if you please."

I wrapped my fingers around the ball. I didn't want to make Doubleday look bad, especially when he was so depressed. I decided to go easy on him and let him hit the ball. I tossed it in underhand, the way you would with a little kid.

But Doubleday didn't even look like he knew how to hold the bat. It was the worst stance I had ever seen. He took a totally pathetic check swing at my first pitch and missed it.

"Strike one!" called the ump.

"There you go, lad," one of the players yelled to me.

"Good swing, sir," I lied. "You're a natural at this game. Next time follow through."

I threw the next pitch even softer. This time, Doubleday took a big, wild swing at it. He spun all the way around and fell on his butt. I wanted to laugh, but I didn't dare.

"Strike two!"

"Keep your eye on the ball, sir," I suggested. "Don't try to kill it. Nice and easy."

I lobbed the next one in right over the plate, as soft as I possibly could. Any six-year-old could have hit it.

But Abner Doubleday couldn't.

"Strike three!" the ump yelled. "You're out, sir!"

"Hip, hip, huzzah!" some of the fielders yelled. "Hip, hip, huzzah!"

"What do you mean, I'm out?" Doubleday shouted. "I just got here!"

"Three strikes and you're out, sir," the umpire said. "That's the rule of the game."

"Well, it's a stupid game!" Doubleday hollered, throwing his bat on the ground.

We all watched as he stormed off into the woods and disappeared. It reminded me of that scene in the movie *Field of Dreams* when the players walked into the cornfield.

When Doubleday was out of earshot, all the players started chuckling. I had to admit, it was pretty funny. My grandmother could hit better than that.

"What a muffin!" one of the players hooted.

I was starting to enjoy myself out there. Even if some of the rules were different, it was still baseball. The outfielders were called "scouts," and they called the shortstop "short scout." It wasn't called a run when you crossed home plate; it was an "ace." I was having fun learning the different rules and terms of the game.

But the fun was about to end.

Suddenly I heard a high-pitched whistling sound from above. I looked up instinctively, just in time to see something flying over the trees and arching down toward our field.

"Sakes alive!" somebody screamed.

Whatever it was, it landed about twenty yards to the right of me, between third base and home plate. A huge ball of fire shot out of the ground, and the boom of the explosion echoed off the trees. Dirt and grass and stuff went flying everywhere. I dove for the dirt.

"Looks like our fun is over, boys," one of the players shouted. "Time to start fightin' again."

13

When Joey Comes Marching Home

A FEW SECONDS AFTER THE SHELL EXPLODED NEAR THE third-base line, a second one hit the ground near first base, sending up another shower of dirt and mud and grass.

"Run for it!" one of the players yelled. My new friends ran for the cover of the woods.

"Joey, we've got to get out of here!" my mother shouted from the little ridge where she was sitting.

"You ain't kidding!" I screamed.

But by now, shells were falling all around the field. I couldn't imagine that anyone was aiming for this empty field. Why waste the ammunition? Probably the Confederates were trying to hit Cemetery Ridge, but their artillery overshot the mark.

I was afraid to run in any direction, because if I

went left and one of those shells landed to the left of me, I might get hurt in a big way—like dead.

The safest strategy, I decided, was to zigzag across the grass. That's what I did, cutting back and forth like a football running back. But instead of dodging tacklers, I was dodging bombs.

Finally I reached Mom, and we hugged each other with relief, fear, and, okay, affection even. I pulled the pack of baseball cards out of my pocket and ripped it open as quickly as I could. The shells were still exploding in the field in front of us. It was getting dark out now. It looked like a fireworks display, except that we were sitting a *bit* too close.

"Hurry, Joey!" Mom said.

I pulled out one of the baseball cards. Mom held my hand. I waited for the tingling sensation to buzz my fingertips.

Then I realized I forgot something. I dropped the card on the grass.

"What is it?" Mom asked.

"My baseball!" I said. "I forgot the baseball that Abner Doubleday signed for me!"

We looked out at the field. The baseball was still lying there on the grass, midway between first and second base.

"Forget about the baseball!" Mom said. "It's not important!"

"It's important to *me*!" I said.

Mom tried to hold me back, but there was no stopping me. I ran back out to the field again. It would only take me a few seconds to grab the ball and run back to Mom.

I was about twenty feet from the ball when a shell landed between first and second base. There was a tremendous explosion of sound and fire. I dove for the ground. Dirt and rocks rained down on me. I looked up to see where the baseball was.

In the exact spot where the ball had been a few seconds earlier, there was now a crater in the ground about the size of a Volkswagen. Maybe getting that ball wasn't so important after all.

"Joey, come back!" hollered Mom.

The baseball was gone. There was no point in searching for it. It probably didn't exist anymore. My dad would be mad that I hadn't brought back an authentic Abner Doubleday–signed baseball, but I had done the best I could.

I sat back down on the grass next to Mom, picked up the baseball card again, and held my mom's hand. I closed my eyes and thought about going home to Louisville.

"Do you feel anything?" Mom asked. "That tingling sensation?"

"Not yet," I replied.

Shells were still falling in the field in front of us. If one of those guys aiming the cannons moved the barrel just one or two degrees up or down, I realized, Mom and I would be dead.

"Hurry up!" Mom said urgently. "They're getting closer!"

"It's hard to concentrate," I said. "There's so much noise. I can't focus."

And then, suddenly, the shelling stopped. All was quiet. I opened my eyes and looked up in the sky just to make sure. It was dark now, except for a big full moon and more stars than I had ever seen in my life. It was beautiful.

There were no city lights to obscure the view of the stars. The electric light hadn't been invented yet, I realized. Neither had the automobile. There was no pollution to get in the way of the stars. I had never seen a sky like this one.

I closed my eyes again and thought about how nice it would be to go back home to Louisville. Riding my bike along the banks of the Ohio River to Waterfront Park and looking across the river to Indiana. Going to the Louisville Slugger Museum. Hanging out at Flip's Fan Club and listening to Flip tell his old baseball stories.

Gradually, the first tingles began to buzz my fingertips.

Out beyond the trees, I could hear music very faintly. There were bugles and fifes and harmonicas playing, but mostly it was just men singing. "When Johnny Comes Marching Home." "The Battle Hymn of the Republic."

It was all quite soothing. I started to feel a little drowsy, but the tingles were getting stronger now, and they kept me awake as they traveled up my arms.

In the distance all the music stopped, except for one lone bugler playing "Taps" very slowly. I knew the tune well, because ever since I was a baby my mother used to sing it to me each night after she put me to bed and turned off the light. The real words were . . .

Day is done.
Gone the sun.
From the lakes,
From the trees,
From the sky . . .

But my mom always sang . . .

Day is done.
We had fun.

Then she would say good night and close the door.

The tingling sensation swept across my chest now and was moving down my stomach toward my legs. I'm sure Mom felt it too. There was no turning back.

I heard footsteps approaching and then a voice, but I kept my eyes closed.

"What are you doing here?" a man asked. "Get your gun! Take shelter! If we're going to win this war, we're going to need every man."

"No, you won't," I said.

And with that, we faded away.

14

A Silly Baseball Game

I WAS PLAYING THIRD BASE. THE MAIN STREET Ophthalmologists had runners on first and second, and there was only one out. Last inning. Their biggest guy was coming up to the plate, holding that huge bat he swings around like a toothpick just to intimidate pitchers. If he got an extra base hit and the two base runners scored, that would tie it up and Flip's Fan Club would have blown a four-run lead. And if he hit one out of the park, well, that would be the ball game.

But I really didn't care.

Well, I wanted us to win and all, but I just couldn't keep my mind on the game.

After all, it was just a silly baseball game. The night before, I had been a witness to one of the most important events in American history. I had seen men kill. I had seen men die! I had seen things I would never forget for the rest of my life. A Little League game between Flip's Fan Club and the Main Street Ophthalmologists just didn't seem all that important anymore.

"Come on, Johnny!" Flip Valentini called from the dugout. "Strike this guy out!"

I hadn't made any really stupid errors or anything. But I'd missed the chance to complete a double play in the third inning. That had cost us a run. And in my three chances at bat, I had fouled out, popped out, and struck out. I wasn't helping the team.

Johnny struck out the big guy. Two outs. Good. One more out and we could go home.

I scanned the bleachers for my mother, but she wasn't around. Where was she? This was the second game in a row that Mom had missed. I was starting to worry about her. What if something had happened to her?

I never used to worry about my mother. She was always the one who had to worry about *me*. But when I scooped her up at Gettysburg and carried her across Cemetery Ridge, something changed. It was the first time I had to protect her instead of the other way around. Someday, when I'm a grown-up and Mom is an old lady, I might have to take care of her all the time, the same way she takes care of Uncle Wilbur.

Why was I thinking about that *now*? I just about slapped myself in the face with my glove. We were in danger of losing this game, and here I was, daydreaming about such weird stuff.

"Two outs!" the coach of the Ophthalmologists hollered. "Run on anything."

Johnny went into his windup, and the batter cracked a sharp grounder down the third-base line. Somehow, my instincts took over. I dove for the ball and managed to get in front of it. The ball bounced off my chest and I scrambled to grab it.

Usually, before every pitch, I mentally rehearse exactly what I'll do if the ball is hit to me. But for the moment, I had forgotten the situation. I had been daydreaming. I didn't remember where the base runners were. I could always throw the ball to first, but it was a long throw and I didn't know if I could get the ball there in time to beat the runner.

"Touch third, Stosh!" everybody was screaming. "Touch third!"

Of course! There were runners at first and second. There was a force play at third.

I rolled over and stabbed at the third-base bag with the ball. I got my hand in there just before the runner from second slid in.

"Yer out!" shouted the umpire.

We won the game, but I had nothing to do with it. The other guys carried the team. I was lucky I had stopped that grounder. If it had gotten past me, both runners would have scored. I was lucky the guys told me what to do with the ball too. I was out of it.

"Are you okay, Stosh?" Flip Valentini asked me

as he drove me home after the game.

"Yeah, sure," I said. "Why?"

"Your head didn't seem to be in the game today."

"It wasn't," I admitted.

"I noticed that you jumped a little with every crack of the bat too," he said. "And when that car backfired back on Whitherspoon Street, you just about jumped through my sunroof."

I guess he was right. Ever since I'd gotten back from Gettysburg, loud sounds had startled me. There had just been so many explosions! Every time I heard a loud noise, it reminded me of the battle. It was crazy, but I almost felt like there were sharpshooters up in the tall buildings of downtown Louisville pointing their rifles at me.

As we got closer to my house, I remembered that Flip was the reason I went to Gettysburg in the first place.

"Hey, guess who I bumped into yesterday," I teased Flip.

"I give up."

"Abner Doubleday."

"Get outta here!" Flip said, driving off the road and stopping the car. Luckily there was just gravel on the shoulder so he could pull over.

"Yup," I said, "and I asked him if he invented baseball."

Flip looked at me expectantly. I must admit, it was fun keeping him in suspense for a few seconds.

"So it worked, huh?" Flip asked. "You were able to do it with a photograph?"

"Yup."

"So?"

"So what?"

"Did Doubleday really invent baseball?" he asked, his eyes twinkling.

It would have been cruel to make him wait any longer.

"Nope," I told him. "He hardly knew *anything* about baseball. He didn't even know that three strikes made an out!"

I told Flip how Doubleday had showed up at the baseball game. When he heard that I'd struck out "the inventor of baseball" on three soft underhand pitches, Flip threw back his head and laughed until tears were running down his cheeks. He was really enjoying himself.

Soon we got back on the road and drove to my house. Flip popped the latch on the trunk so I could get my duffel bag out. He made me promise to tell him all about Gettysburg on Thursday.

"What's Thursday?" I asked.

"How could you forget?" Flip said. "We're playin' your buddy Bobby Fuller's team. I know how you and Fuller get along real good."

I pulled my stuff out of the trunk and made a promise to myself that on Thursday my head would be in the game and not worrying about Mom or anything else.

"Hey Flip," I asked after he rolled down the window. "Do your children take care of you?"

"Never had any kids," Flip said. "Never found the

right girl to marry. Guess I'll just have to take care of myself."

As he pulled away from the curb, Flip flipped a pack of baseball cards out the window to me.

"You might want to go meet some of these guys next," he said with a laugh.

I caught the pack of cards. That's when I realized something. The trip to Gettysburg had been my last. My time-traveling days were over.

I had been fooling my mother for a while, telling her how these trips were nothing more than educational, like school field trips to the past. I never told her about the times I was nearly killed.

But now that Mom had joined me for a trip, the jig was up. There was no way she would ever let me do something so reckless again.

And to be honest about it, I didn't want to travel through time again anyway. Mom was right. The more I did it, the higher the probability that something terrible would happen. Eventually my luck would run out. One of those bullets would find me one day. Or something would happen and I wouldn't be able to get back home.

I may be a little crazy, but I'm not stupid.

When I opened the front door, Uncle Wilbur was watching one of those dopey TV court shows where people argue about dumb stuff and a judge decides who is right. Uncle Wilbur smiled at me and asked me the score of my game.

Mom was in the kitchen, sitting at the computer

table in the corner. Books and papers were scattered around the table.

"Joey!" she said, looking up as if I had surprised her. When she saw me in my uniform, she must have suddenly remembered she missed my game again.

"Are you okay, Mom?" I asked.

"I lost track of the time," she explained. "I didn't even go to the hospital today. I'm sorry, Joey."

Wow, my mother *never* takes a day off from work. She must have been working on something really important. Taxes, I figured.

"What are you doing, Mom?" I asked.

"Planning a trip," she said. There was sudden excitement in her voice.

"Are we going to Disney World?" I asked. My mother had been telling me she would take me to Florida ever since I was little, and now I was almost too old.

"No, we're going to Washington, D.C."

I leaned over and noticed that one of the papers on the table was a map of Washington.

"Cool," I said. "Can we go to the Air and Space Museum?"

"No, the Air and Space Museum won't be built yet," she said.

"Huh?"

"Joey, we're going to Washington in 1865," she said excitedly. Her eyes were shining. "We're going to save Abraham Lincoln's life!"

15

The Plan

MAYBE THERE WAS SOMETHING WRONG WITH MY HEARing, I thought. My ears were clogged with wax or something.

Nah, that couldn't be it.

Maybe I had entered a parallel universe. You know, one of those sci-fi worlds where everything that happens is opposite from the universe we live in.

Nah, that couldn't be it either.

There was only one possible explanation for what Mom had just said to me.

My mother had gone insane.

After getting shot at, covered with blood, and very nearly killed at the Battle of Gettysburg, my mother wanted to go back in time with me *again* to stop a bullet before it got to Abraham Lincoln? This, from a woman who won't even let me ride my bike into downtown Louisville by myself.

It was crazy. It was impossible.

On the other hand, maybe Mom just wanted to go back in time so she could pick up that Medal of Honor that Abner Doubleday said he was going to recommend her for!

In any case, my mother had a look in her eye that I hadn't seen in years, not since before she and my dad broke up. It was the gleam of energy and excitement. She even looked younger to me.

"I had a brainstorm when we were back at Gettysburg," she told me, gesturing with her hands. "It came to me while you were playing baseball with those Union soldiers. The idea popped into my head that we could go back in time together and prevent President Lincoln from being assassinated!"

"Mom—"

"Hear me out, Joey," she said, opening one of the library books in front of her. "Almost two years after the Battle of Gettysburg, on April 14, 1865, Lincoln was shot by John Wilkes Booth at Ford's Theatre in Washington. All we have to do is get a photograph that was taken in Washington that day. Then we can go back and stop Booth before he gets to Lincoln!"

"*This* is what you've been doing all day?" I asked. Every book on the table was about Abraham Lincoln, I could see now. Up on the computer screen was a website called thedaylincolndied.com.

"I couldn't sleep last night," Mom said. "I was up until four o'clock in the morning figuring everything out. I couldn't go to work today. This is more important."

"Mom, you're obsessed!"

"Look at this," she said, pointing to a timeline on the screen. "All the facts are here. At exactly 8:30 P.M., the president and his wife, Mary, arrived at Ford's Theatre to see a play called *Our American Cousin*. John Wilkes Booth arrived at 9:30 P.M.—one hour later. He had a single-shot derringer pistol and a hunting knife with him. Booth tied up his horse in an alley behind the theater, and then he went to the Star Saloon next door. He had a drink in the saloon. At 10:07, he entered the theater. Eight minutes later, he shot the president. Lincoln clung to life through the night and died at 7:22 A.M. the next morning. It's all here, Joey."

"And your plan is?" I was almost afraid to hear what scheme she was cooking up.

"When Booth is in the saloon, it will be the perfect opportunity to nail him," she said.

I still couldn't believe it. Before Gettysburg my mother had been the most cautious person in the world. She never did *anything* risky or dangerous. She would take a first aid kit with her when she went grocery shopping. One of the biggest problems she ever had with my dad was that he liked to gamble. And now she comes up with this wacky plan to prevent the Lincoln assassination? It was crazy.

"What are you going to do, *shoot* John Wilkes Booth?" I asked, knowing full well that my mother was passionately antiviolence and had never fired a gun in her life.

"No," she said. "I don't need to *kill* him. I just

need to stop him."

My mother pulled out a little gadget from the desk drawer. It looked sort of like that electric razor the barber uses to trim the hair on the back of your neck.

"It's a stun gun," she said. "It doesn't shoot bullets. It shoots a high-voltage electrical charge. See?"

She pushed a button, and a scary-looking blue spark flicked across the top of the stun gun. It made a crackling noise too. It was like something out of *Star Trek*.

"That's cool!" I said. "Can I borrow it? There are some kids at school I'd like to try it out on."

"Very funny," Mom said. "We keep a few of them at the hospital just in case a patient goes crazy and we have to subdue him."

"How's it work?"

"You touch it against somebody and it sends two hundred thousand volts of electricity through their skin. Their muscles and nerves are immobilized for a few minutes. They're confused and imbalanced. You zap somebody with one of these and believe me, they'll be in no condition to assassinate anybody. It even works through clothing."

"I have one question." I asked, "Have you lost your marbles?"

Uncle Wilbur wheeled himself into the kitchen, opened up the refrigerator door, and peered inside. His hearing isn't very good, but Mom lowered her voice anyway.

"It will be a simple operation," my mother whispered. "In and out. We zap Booth with the stun gun, turn him over to the police, and then we come home. It won't be at all like Gettysburg."

Uncle Wilbur closed the refrigerator door without taking anything and wheeled himself back to the living room.

"You make it sound like *Mission: Impossible*, Mom," I said. "It's never simple. Time travel doesn't always work out the way you think it will."

"But it's worth the risk," she said. "Think of what we can accomplish! Lincoln was probably America's greatest president. Who knows what would have happened if he had lived. We can change the entire course of American history!"

"There's the chance that we could make things worse, too, you know," I countered. "There's no way to know for sure if things would have been better with Lincoln alive."

My mother paused for a moment, letting out a sigh.

"Joey, before we went to Gettysburg, I never did anything outrageous in my life. Let's face it, my life is pretty ordinary. But being at Gettysburg was an amazing experience. It made me feel so *alive*. I want to do it again. I want to do some good in the world."

"You save lives every day," I reminded her. "That's doing something good."

"I want to save *Lincoln's* life."

"Mom, you could get killed! What if Booth pulls out his gun and shoots you? He's an assassin! What if he stabs you with that hunting knife?"

"I'll stun him before he has the chance," Mom said. "He won't suspect me. His guard won't be up."

Maybe I *was* in a parallel universe. All the other times, it was me arguing that I wanted to travel through time and it was *Mom* thinking up all the reasons why I shouldn't do it. Now everything was backward.

Every argument I made, she gave me one back. She was determined to do this thing. I was running out of reasons why it was a bad idea.

"You'll never find a photo that was taken in Washington on the same day Lincoln was shot."

"I can try."

"Look, Mom," I said. "Remember when I went back to 1919 and tried to prevent the Black Sox Scandal? I couldn't do it. You won't be able to do this either. It says in all the history books that Abraham Lincoln was assassinated by John Wilkes Booth on that night. There's nothing that you or anyone can do about that now. You can't change history."

Uncle Wilbur rolled back into the kitchen and opened the refrigerator again.

"When's dinner?" he muttered. "I'm starved."

Mom looked over at Uncle Wilbur, then looked at me, raising one eyebrow.

"Can't change history, eh?" she asked.

It looked like I would be going to 1865 to try to save the life of Abraham Lincoln.

16

Early Dismissal

A COUPLE OF DAYS WENT BY, AND MY MOTHER DIDN'T mention her wacky plan to go back to 1865 and save the life of Abraham Lincoln.

Life returned to normal. I went back to school. Mom went back to work. Uncle Wilbur watched his dopey TV shows. My dad came over to visit. He was a little mad that I hadn't brought him back a baseball signed by Abner Doubleday. But when I told him what we had been through at Gettysburg, he said he understood.

I was beginning to think Mom had forgotten about the Lincoln assassination. But then, I was sitting in social studies on Wednesday afternoon when Mrs. Van Hook came over to me and told me I should report to the office.

Being called down to the office is not usually a good thing. It's not as serious as being called down to the principal's office, but chances are that if you have to report to *any* school office, it's not good news. I couldn't think of anything I had done that would have gotten me into trouble, at least recently.

"What did I do?" I asked Mrs. Van Hook, but she just shrugged.

I went down to the school office, and Mom was sitting there waiting for me. She had a mischievous grin on her face.

"What is it?" I asked. "Am I in trouble?"

Mom pulled a photo out of a large envelope and showed it to me. She had that wild gleam in her eye.

The unfinished Washington Monument

"I got it from the Library of Congress," she said.

"So?"

"Joey, it's the Washington Monument . . . under construction!"

"Mom, I'm in the middle of social studies class."

"Oh, who cares about social studies?" she said. "The Washington Monument is just six blocks from Ford's Theatre, Joey! This is the picture I've been searching for!"

The school secretary looked up at us from her desk.

"How do you know when this picture was taken?" I said, lowering my voice. "It could have been years after the assassination. Then it's no use."

Mom flipped the photo over. On the back were these words:

WASHINGTON MONUMENT, APRIL 14, 1865

"This is it, Joey!" Mom bubbled. "This is our ticket. You can do it. You can save Lincoln's life. Nobody else can do it."

"Mom, I have a math quiz seventh period," I moaned.

"Oh, forget about your math quiz!" Mom said. "We have the chance to change American history! Let's go!"

She practically dragged me out of school. There was no getting around it. I was going to go back in time and try to prevent the Lincoln assassination.

"What about Uncle Wilbur?" I asked as Mom

drove—a little too fast—home from school.

"He's taking his afternoon nap," she said. "I told him to fix himself some dinner when he wakes up. He'll be fine."

When we got home, all the stuff we would need was already laid out carefully on the coffee table in the living room. Stun gun. First aid kit. Snacks. Map of Washington. Umbrella. Old-time money so Mom could buy a drink at the Star Saloon. She'd gotten a new pack of baseball cards so we would be able to get home. She fit everything into her purse except the umbrella. Mom even got some goofy-looking antique clothes so would could blend in on the streets of Washington. We put them on and sat on the couch together.

"Are you ready?" she said excitedly as she took out the photo of the Washington Monument.

"I'm scared, Mom," I admitted.

"What are you scared of, Joey?"

"What if something goes wrong?"

"Like what?"

"Well, what if we do save Lincoln?" I said, thinking out loud. "And history is changed? We can't predict how the world will be different if Lincoln had lived. Maybe horrible things will happen. Maybe we'll come back home and find out our house was never built. Or maybe, because of some weird chain of events, we'll come back home and find out America doesn't exist anymore, or everybody is speaking German, or the whole world has been destroyed by atomic bombs. What if we come back and find out that you were never born? That would mean I was never born. Then what would happen?"

Mom thought it over.

"I'm willing to take that chance if you are," she said.

I took the photo in one hand and held Mom's hand with the other. I thought about what Washington, D.C., would look like in 1865. I didn't even know if the White House had been built yet.

"Do you really have to bring an umbrella?" I mumbled.

"It might be raining in Washington."

Soon the tingling sensation started to buzz across my fingertips. It raced up my arms, down my legs, and all over my body. Just as I felt myself starting to fade away, I dropped the photo, grabbed the stupid umbrella out of Mom's hand and tossed it aside.

And then we disappeared.

17

Unexpected Company

WHEN I OPENED MY EYES, THERE IT WAS—THE Washington Monument. It looked exactly the same as it did in the photo, except it was dark out, and there were people all around. For once, I had traveled through time and landed at the exact spot I had been aiming for. Things were looking good.

"Let's go," Mom said. "We don't have a lot of time."

"How will you know when you see John Wilkes Booth?" I asked as she grabbed my hand. "There could be a lot of guys standing around that bar."

"I downloaded pictures of him from the Internet," she said. "I know exactly what he looks like. He's about five eight, dark hair, mustache, very handsome."

John Wilkes Booth

The streets of Washington looked like a big outdoor festival. Horses and buggies were taking people everywhere. Men were all dressed up in old-time clothes and hats and women were in fancy dresses. Everybody seemed happy.

"The Civil War ended just five days ago," Mom told me as she led me across Constitution Avenue. "It was almost exactly four years ago today that the whole thing started. That's why everybody's celebrating."

Mom had learned just about everything there was to know about the Lincoln assassination. She had even memorized how we would get from the

Washington Monument to 10th Street, where Ford's Theatre was located. She was walking quickly, pulling me along by the hand.

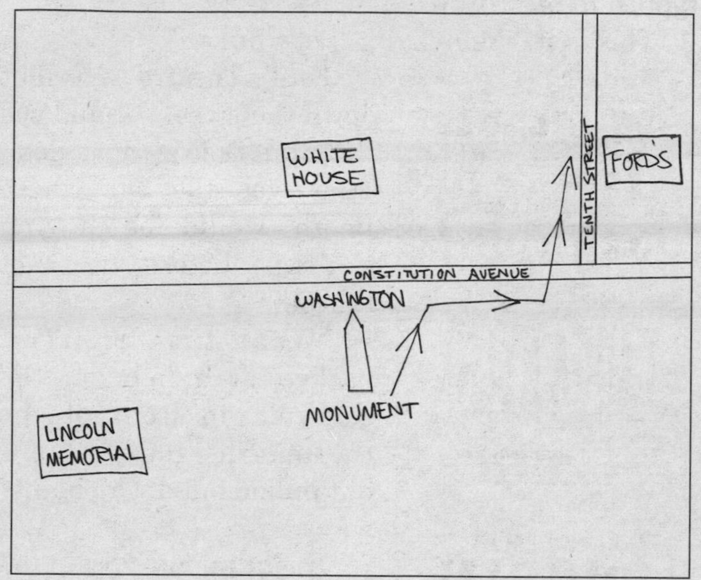

Mom knew we didn't have time to waste. She had mapped out the route to Ford's Theatre.

"Can you tell me what time it is?" she asked an older man in a top hat.

"Nearly ten o'clock," he said, after taking a watch out of his pocket.

"Oh no!" Mom said. "We might be late!"

We were running now, but it was hard to make progress because Constitution Avenue was choked with people and horses. Mom was just about shoving people out of the way so we could get by them.

Finally we reached 10th Street. I was out of breath. There was a flyer lying in the street, and I stopped to pick it up.

"This is it!" Mom said. "Let's hurry!"

FORD'S THEATRE

TENTH STREET, ABOVE E.

Friday Evening, April 14th, 1865

BENEFIT!

—AND—

LAST NIGHT

OF MISS

LAURA KEENE

MR. JOHN DYOTT

AND

MR. HARRY HAWK.

TOM TAYLOR'S CELEBRATED ECCENTRIC COMEDY,

ONE THOUSAND NIGHTS,

ENTITLED

OUR AMERICAN

COUSIN

FLORENCE TRENCHARD.......MISS LAURA KEENE

Abel Murcott, Clerk to Attorney..........John Dyott

Asa Trenchard..........Harry Hawk

SATURDAY EVENING, APRIL 15,

BENEFIT of Miss JENNIE GOURLAY

THE OCTOROON

EDWIN ADAMS

THE PRICES OF ADMISSION:

J. R. FORD, Business Manager.

Program used at Ford's Theatre on the night Lincoln was shot

Ford's Theatre was right down the street. I could see the Star Saloon next door. That was the bar where Booth would be having a drink before he shot Lincoln.

"What time is it?" I barked at a lady on the sidewalk in front of the theater. She glared at me, but pulled out a watch anyway.

"Eight minutes past ten," she said. "But you should get some manners, young man."

"We're late!" Mom exclaimed, pulling me toward the front door of the theater. "Booth went inside one minute ago! We'll have to change plans! He's going to shoot the president in seven minutes!"

A guy in a uniform was standing in the doorway, his arms crossed in front of his chest.

"We need two tickets, please," Mom said as politely as she could, under the circumstances. She pulled some money out of her purse. "And hurry, please."

"We're sold out tonight, ma'am," the man said. "Not a seat left for tonight's show. Mr. Lincoln is here, you know."

"I know," Mom said hurriedly. "We don't mind standing."

"No standing room, ma'am."

"This is an emergency!" Mom said.

"A *national* emergency," I added.

"I'm sorry," the guy said, unimpressed. "I suggest you come back tomorrow. A new play called *The Octoroon* is opening. We'll have plenty of seats once the president is gone."

"I'm sure you will," Mom snapped. "Look, did a man just come in here about a minute ago? Handsome guy? Mustache, bushy dark hair?"

"Sure. I seen him."

"Did *he* have a ticket?" Mom demanded.

"No."

"Then why did you let *him* in?"

"He is a very highly regarded actor," the guy said. "He comes here all the time. That was Mr. John Wilkes Booth."

Mom and I looked at each other in a panic. It figured. Here we were trying to save the president's life, and we weren't allowed inside the theater. But the guy who is going to *kill* the president can waltz right in the front door, no questions asked. Life wasn't fair.

We had five minutes, tops, to save Lincoln. I thought about trying to take a run at the guy and bowl him over, but he was a lot bigger than me. Mom grabbed my hand and pulled me down the steps.

We ran around to the side of the theater. There was a dark alley there, with a horse tied up to a post. I looked around desperately for a fire escape I could climb onto and sneak into the theater, but I guess they didn't have fire escapes back in 1865.

"Joey! Look! A door!"

I was about to pull the large wooden door open when suddenly a man stepped out of the shadows and grabbed me.

"Hold it right there!" he said.

I turned around and gasped. I couldn't believe what I saw.

It was Abner Doubleday.

I didn't recognize him at first because he wasn't wearing an army uniform.

"What are *you* doing in Washington, General Doubleday?" Mom asked. She was smiling nervously, almost like she was flirting with him.

"I work here," Doubleday said. "A better question is what are *you* doing in Washington? Don't I know you two from somewhere?"

"Yes, we met at Gettysburg, sir. Two years ago. I'm a nurse. You mentioned something about the

Medal of Honor. But I really don't have time to discuss that right now. It's very important that my son and I get inside the theater right away."

"That won't be possible," Doubleday said.

"Why not?" I asked.

"Because I'm placing the two of you under arrest."

"What for?" Mom asked.

"For the attempted assassination of President Lincoln."

"What?"

"There have been rumors circulating that a conspiracy is afoot to kill the president," Doubleday said as he grabbed Mom by the shoulder. "It said in the newspaper that Mr. Lincoln would attend the play this evening. So I decided to stop by the theater in case there was any trouble. It looks like I found some."

"You've got it all wrong!" Mom said desperately. "We came here tonight for the same reason you did. We're trying to *prevent* the assassination! The assassin entered the theater just a few minutes ago! And we only have a few minutes before he is going to shoot the president! We *must* get inside!"

"You seem to know an awful lot about this plot," Doubleday said calmly. "Obviously, you must be in on it."

"We're not in on it!" I shouted. "We're trying to *stop* it!"

"I suspected something about you two back in

Gettysburg," Doubleday said. "I recall you were wearing a bizarre nurse's uniform, and you could not name your regiment. And the boy here proposed some preposterous notion that I invented the game of baseball. Obviously, both of you are lunatics, and possibly dangerous. The president will thank me when he learns that I apprehended you. Perhaps I will finally be reinstated to my rightful command."

"General Doubleday, if you don't let us in this door *right now*, the president is going to get killed!" Mom yelled. "He won't be able to thank you for anything!"

"Tell it to the police," he said, pulling us down the alley toward the street. "You two have some explaining to do."

The sound of audience laughter could be heard from inside the theater. I saw Mom reach into her purse for something. I wasn't sure what it was at first, but then I saw it.

The stun gun.

"Do it, Mom!"

Bzzzzzzzzzzttttttttt!

Doubleday froze for a moment, just looking at us. His eyes got really big and his hair stood on end. Then he slumped to the ground and hit the dirt like a sack of potatoes.

"Let's go!" Mom said.

She was about to pull open the door when a gunshot echoed into the alley, followed by a woman screaming.

18

The Escape

IT WAS TOO LATE. PRESIDENT LINCOLN HAD BEEN SHOT.

The door we were about to open was suddenly pushed open from the inside, and almost slammed me in the head. A man charged out, his eyes wild, and a grimace of pain on his face. He was waving a knife around.

"Make way!"

It was obviously John Wilkes Booth. He ran out the door with a pronounced limp and almost tripped over Doubleday, who was lying still on the ground. Booth untied the horse and galloped away.

"We've got to stop him!" I shouted.

"Don't bother," Mom said wearily. "I know what will happen to him. They'll hunt him down. Twelve days from now, they'll shoot him in a Virginia barn. They don't need any help from us."

Mom was leaning against the wall, like she was too tired and depressed to stand up. She looked like she might break down in tears.

I couldn't let it end like that. She had tried so hard to prevent the assassination. We weren't failures. If it hadn't been for Abner Doubleday, we might have saved the president. I put my arm around Mom and held her. And suddenly, I got an idea.

"Maybe you can still save Lincoln," I said. "Couldn't you do your lifesaving stuff on him or something?"

Mom rested her head on my shoulder for a moment without saying a word. Then she lifted it, and her eyes were bright again.

"You're right!" she said. "Lincoln isn't dead yet! He won't die until tomorrow morning!"

"Right!"

"The bullet was only a half inch in diameter," she said excitedly. "It entered slightly above his left ear in the back of his head and it was lodged behind his right eye. The doctors won't know that until after he's dead. But I know it *now*. Maybe I can save him!"

"Yeah!"

Mom pulled out her first aid kit. We stepped over Doubleday and rushed out into the street. There was already a crowd forming in front of the theater.

"The president has been shot!" people were shouting.

In seconds, it was pandemonium. Women started screaming. Men started weeping. People started pushing, pointing, shoving, yelling, and bumping into each other. We couldn't get to the front of Ford's Theatre.

The front doors finally opened and four or five men came out carrying a stretcher. The only part of Lincoln I could see at first was his shoes.

"They're going to carry him to that house over there!" Mom said, pulling me across the street. "I've got to get inside."

"Clear a passage!" yelled one of the men carrying the stretcher.

As Mom and I struggled to get past the people crowding the street, I caught a glimpse of Abraham Lincoln's face. His eyes were closed. There was blood on his head. He was a very tall man, and he barely fit on the stretcher. One limp arm was dangling down, almost touching the street.

"The carriage ride to the White House will surely kill him," one of the stretcher-bearers said. "He must be taken to the nearest available bed!"

"Bring him in here!" yelled a man standing in front of the house Mom had pointed out.

There were so many people clogging the street that by the time we got to the front of the house, Lincoln was already inside it.

"I might be able to save him!" Mom yelled to the man who was closing the door behind him.

"I am a doctor, ma'am," he said. "The wound is mortal. It is impossible for him to recover."

"You've got to believe me!" Mom shouted at the guy. "I know things about medicine that you don't know. I know things doctors won't know for more than a hundred years!"

"We will do the best we can, ma'am."

"Please!" Mom begged. "I come from the future! I can help!"

"Lunatic!" the doctor said, and then he slammed the door in Mom's face.

While Mom was arguing with the doctor, I turned around and saw the one thing I really did *not* want to see at that particular moment.

Abner Doubleday.

He looked groggy, staggering across the street like a drunk.

"We gotta get out of here, Mom!" I said. "Doubleday woke up."

"I don't care!" she said, pounding on the door for them to let her in. "I've got to save the president!"

Abner Doubleday looked like he was coming our way.

"Mom!" I shouted. "You zapped him with the stun gun before Lincoln was shot! Doubleday probably thinks we ran in the theater and killed the president!"

"You're right," Mom said. "We'd better get out of here."

"Stop them!" Doubleday hollered as we ran down the steps. "They're the ones who killed the president! The woman is insane, and she has a weapon of some sort!"

I'm not the fastest runner in the world. Mom is no Olympic sprinter either. But we tore out of there so fast, we could have set a world record. A few people chased us for the first fifty yards or so, but then we got lost in the crowd. Just to be on the safe side, we didn't stop running until we were at least a mile away from Ford's Theatre.

We collapsed to the ground, exhausted, under a tree in the middle of a grassy field. Nobody was around. It was actually quite peaceful. The only thing I could hear was my heart pounding.

"Do you know what they did to the people who conspired with Booth to kill Lincoln?" Mom asked me as we caught our breath.

"What?"

"They hanged them," Mom said.

"Let's go home," I suggested.

"Good idea."

She pulled the pack of new baseball cards out of her purse and handed them to me.

"You know what?" Mom asked as I ripped open the wrapper. "I recognize this spot."

"Oh, yeah?" I said. "What is it?"

"This is where they're going to build the Lincoln Memorial."

I took a card from the pack. Mom and I held hands and closed our eyes. I felt a drop of rain hit my head, and then a few more. It wasn't long before the tingling sensation started to flow across my fingertips, down my arms, legs, and throughout my body. The rain was picking up.

"Where's my umbrella?" Mom asked. "I thought I brought my umbrella."

And then we faded away.

19

The Rematch

"HEY STOSHACK! YOUR MOTHER IS A REFRIGERATOR repairman!"

I hate Bobby Fuller. I'm not talking about the kind of hate like when you hate broccoli or hate math class. I'm talking about true, deep-down, wish-somebody-would-die kind of hate. Sometimes I think the world would be such a better place if only people like Bobby Fuller weren't in it.

It was Thursday, and we were playing Fuller's team. The game had just begun, and he didn't waste an inning before he started getting on me. Fortunately, there weren't many parents in the bleachers to listen. It was after school, so I guess a lot of moms and dads were still at work. My mom wasn't there, as usual.

I looked at the first pitch, and the ump called it a strike.

"You can't hit, Stoshack!" Fuller hollered at me

from third base. "Why bother trying? You should take up a sport that suits you better. Like gymnastics."

Be cool, I said to myself. What I really wanted to do was fling the bat aside, charge over to third base, and stomp him into the dirt. But I knew from experience that it wouldn't help me any. I had to try to ignore him.

All he wanted to do was rattle me, throw me off a little. I took a deep breath. I wasn't going to let him do it. The next pitch came in, and I let it go by for ball one.

"We missed you, Stoshack!" Fuller yelled. "We missed you when we were all standing in line for brains and good looks!"

How come nobody ever shuts him up? Why doesn't his coach say something to him? I know that if I ever started harassing somebody on another team, Coach Valentini would pull me aside and tell me to knock it off.

The next pitch sailed over the catcher's mitt and went all the way to the backstop. Ball two. Two and one.

I shifted my left foot over just a little to increase my chance of pulling the ball down the third-base line. The thought briefly flashed through my mind that it would be so cool to hit Bobby Fuller in the head with a line drive.

That's when I hit Bobby Fuller in the head with a line drive.

I didn't mean to, honest. But the pitch was a little inside, and I got around on it pretty good. I hit a rocket right at him. I wasn't even out of the batter's box when I saw him put his glove up, a millisecond too late. The ball bounced off his head and ricocheted about twenty feet straight up in the air.

I didn't stick around to see what happened after that. I was digging for first. Kit Clement, who was coaching there, waved his arms for me to keep going, so I did.

As I was rounding second, I looked up and saw Bobby Fuller. He was flat on his back next to third base, his arms and legs spread out as if he had been making snow angels. He wasn't moving. The ball was sitting on the infield dirt a couple of feet away from him.

This wasn't any decoy. He was really hurt.

"Somebody call a doctor!" Flip Valentini yelled.

I know that when a kid on the other team gets hurt, you're not supposed to help. It's just not cool. You're supposed to stand around quietly and not crack any jokes or anything until the kid looks like he's okay. But Bobby Fuller was just lying there like he was dead. I was the one who hit the ball, so I suppose it was my fault. I was the closest one to him too. So I ran over and knelt beside him.

"Are you okay?" I asked.

No response.

"Don't help him, Stosh," one of the guys on my team yelled. "He's a jerk."

I tilted Bobby's head back with my hand and put my ear to his mouth to listen for breathing. I couldn't hear anything. A bunch of Bobby's teammates had gathered around.

I pinched his nostrils shut with two fingers and opened his mouth with my other hand. Then I covered his mouth with mine and blew some air inside.

"Oh man!" Burton Ernie said. "Stoshack is kissing Fuller!"

"Oh, shut up, Burton!" somebody said.

Fuller's chest went up slightly, and when I took my mouth away it went down again. I took a deep breath and did it again, a little harder.

Suddenly, Bobby opened his eyes. I took my mouth away. He was going to be okay. Everybody on both teams started cheering.

I didn't mean to hit Fuller with the ball, and I didn't mean to save his life or anything. Sometimes you just do things without thinking. Your instincts take over. But at least some good will come of this, I thought to myself. He can't hate me anymore. If I hadn't acted quickly, he might have died. He owed his life to me.

"Get your filthy lips off me, Stoshack!" Fuller said, spitting on the ground and wiping his mouth with his sleeve. "You're a sick freak!"

I didn't know what to do. I never expected him to *like* me, but I thought a little thank-you was in order.

Then Fuller did something that shocked me even more. He picked up the ball lying on the ground near him and tagged me with it.

"You're out, Stoshack!" he said.

"What? You gotta be kidding!"

The umpire came over. Fuller held the ball up to him.

"He's the base runner, right?" Fuller said. "And he isn't on a base. So I tagged him. He's out, right?"

Everybody looked at the ump. He thought it over for a minute, scratching his head.

"The base runner is out," he finally announced.

Well, I went ballistic.

"I came over to *help*!" I shouted at the ump. "I might have saved his *life*! Why didn't you call time-out when I was giving him mouth-to-mouth resuscitation? This is so totally unfair, it's ridiculous!"

"Yer out," said the ump. "I don't change my calls."

Well, I felt like walking off the field. Forever. I felt like giving up baseball. I felt like punching somebody too.

But I didn't do any of those things. Flip Valentini put an arm around me and walked me around the outfield for a few minutes. Flip has a way of calming a guy down. He told me I had done a wonderful thing helping Bobby, even though he was a big jerk. He said he was proud of me. And he told me how much respect I would earn if I would be able to control my temper and come back and play the rest of the game.

So I did.

Bobby Fuller's coach tried to talk him into seeing a doctor to make sure he was okay, but he wouldn't do it. I guess he didn't want to admit he was hurt.

Everybody pretended like the incident never happened. We scored a run in the second inning, and Fuller's team got two in the third. We tied it in the fourth, and they jumped ahead, scoring three runs in the fifth.

Fuller was still yelling things at me, but they were mostly of the "Stoshack, you suck!" variety. Totally unimaginative. That bonk on the head must have scrambled his brains a little, preventing him from thinking up his usual clever zingers.

We were down by three runs when we came up in the sixth inning, the last inning. But they were on their third pitcher, and this kid was not nearly as fast as the first two. Our guys started hitting the ball. Sean Phillips got a single to start things off, and Gabe Radley doubled him home. Then Kit Clement drove Gabe in and suddenly we were just one run down. You could feel the excitement on the bench. We had a rally going. Hitting is contagious.

Kit was on first. It was my turn to hit.

"You suck, Stoshack!" Bobby Fuller yelled at me from third base.

Man, what do you have to do to make somebody like you? Sometimes I feel like just saying to him, "Why don't you like me? What did I ever do to *you*?" But then he'd know I cared. I really didn't want him to know I cared.

I looked over to Flip Valentini, coaching at third. We both knew I would be swinging away. A hit would tie the game, and a homer would win it. I settled into the batter's box and pumped my bat back and forth to get loose. I looked at strike one.

"You suck, Stoshack! You suck you suck you suck you suck . . ."

I didn't want to hit the ball anywhere near Bobby Fuller. Not after what happened in the first inning. I just didn't need that aggravation. Ball one came in.

If I could drop one in down the right-field line, it would tie the game, I thought. I shifted my left leg a little to try to hit the ball in that direction. The next pitch looked good, but I swung through it. Strike two.

The stance felt uncomfortable. I went back to my regular stance. One ball, two strikes. Got to protect the plate. I didn't want to hear what Fuller would say if I struck out.

The next pitch was a little inside, but I felt I had to take a rip at it because the ump might call it strike three. I made contact, and hit a sharp grounder down the third-base line. I didn't hit it hard by any means. Fuller dove for the ball, but he was an inch or two short. The ball skittered past him.

"Go! Go! Go!" everybody started screaming.

I was off with the crack of the bat. Now it was just a matter of how far I could make it. When I turned the corner at first, the ball was still rattling around the left-field corner. Kit scored easily to tie the game. I dug for second and didn't even look for the coach's sign. I was going for third.

"Slide! Slide! Slide!" everybody was screaming.

I slid into third, but I didn't have to. The ball got

past Fuller. The pitcher backed him up, and I stayed where I was.

I asked for time so I could brush the dirt off my pants and examine the situation. The game was tied now. If I could score from third, we'd win it. There was one out. Burton Ernie was up.

"You suck, Stoshack," Fuller informed me.

"What is your problem, man?" I said, unable to restrain myself. "You should really think about getting some counseling or something. You've got problems."

"You're my problem, Stoshack."

"Oh, give it a rest, Fuller."

"You ain't gonna score," Fuller said. "No way you're gonna score."

"Okay, let's go, Burton!" hollered Coach Valentini from the third-base coaching box. "Drive him in. You can do it!"

Burton got himself set in the batter's box. The catcher went out to say a few words to his pitcher. Coach Valentini sidled over to me.

"Stosh," he whispered in my ear, "loosen your belt."

"Huh?" I must have misinterpreted what he said.

"I said loosen your belt. Take the buckle off."

"Why?"

"Just *do* it!"

I opened up my belt buckle, and I didn't figure out why until Burton swung at the first pitch and sent a high fly ball toward centerfield. It wasn't deep, but it was deep enough for me to try to tag up. I scurried back to get my foot on the third-base bag. When the ball was caught, I broke for home.

I knew I was going to be sliding no matter what. I hit the dirt, and the catcher slapped the tag on me.

"Safe!" the ump hollered, and everybody on our bench came out to mob me.

"Hey look!" Burton shouted. He was pointing toward third base.

Bobby Fuller was standing there. And he was holding my belt in his hand.

"You done good, Stosh," Flip said when he dropped me off at home. "I'm proud of you. You should be proud of yourself too."

I was, come to think of it. I couldn't wait to tell Mom that I had saved somebody's life, even if it was that jerk Bobby Fuller, who didn't deserve to live anyway.

She was hunched over the computer in the kitchen when I walked in.

"Mom, you won't believe what happened!" I bubbled. "I hit a line drive off Bobby Fuller's head, and he might have died if I hadn't given him mouth-to-mouth resuscitation just like you showed me. And then I scored the winning run because Flip told me to loosen my belt, and after I crossed the plate Bobby Fuller was standing there with my belt in his hand and it was so cool—"

"Joey," Mom said, looking up from the screen, "did you know that President Lincoln had a secretary named Kennedy, and President Kennedy had a secretary named Lincoln?"

"Huh?"

"I was looking at this website," she continued. "Check this out. Lincoln took office in 1861 and Kennedy took office in 1961. There are fifteen letters in John Wilkes Booth and fifteen letters in Lee Harvey Oswald, the guy who shot Kennedy."

"So?"

"There's more. Booth ran from a theater to a warehouse, and Oswald ran from a warehouse to a theater. And get *this*. Lincoln was shot in Ford's Theatre and Kennedy was shot while he was riding in a Lincoln automobile, which is made by—are you ready for this—*Ford*!"

She looked up at me, that devilish gleam in her eye. "Doesn't that strike you as curious?"

"No!" I said, backing away from her.

"What?" she said, all innocent.

"I am *not* going to go back and try to prevent the Kennedy assassination!"

"But Joey, it would be so *simple*," Mom said. "All we have to do is get to the Texas School Book Depository building in Dallas, Texas, on November 22nd, 1963. It won't be like the Lincoln thing at *all*. There were plenty of photos taken that day. Please?"

"No!" I said. "And that's final!"

Facts and Fictions

Everything in this book is true, except for the stuff I made up. It's only fair to tell you which is which.

Abner Doubleday was a real person. He was born in 1819 and grew up in Cooperstown, New York, which is the main reason why the Baseball Hall of Fame is located there. While many people think of him as the inventor of baseball, historians agree it is a myth.

But Doubleday *was* an American hero. He graduated from West Point in 1842 and quickly advanced through the ranks of the United States Army. He aimed the first Union shot at Fort Sumter, which started the Civil War. He led troops in the battles of Antietam, South Mountain, Fredericksburg, Chancellorsville, and, of course, Gettysburg.

At Gettysburg, Doubleday took command of First Corps after General John Reynolds was killed on the first day of fighting. But that night Doubleday was replaced when it was reported that his division ran from the battlefield at the first contact with Confederate forces. Even though it wasn't true, he was demoted and ordered back to Washington.

Humiliated, Doubleday said he would leave the army if he was not reinstated. He wasn't, so he did. He took a low-level desk job working for the government in Washington. That's where he was when Abraham Lincoln was assassinated. Doubleday was *not* at Ford's Theatre on the night of Lincoln's assassination. I made up that part. But all other facts about the assassination are accurate.

Doubleday died from Bright's disease at age seventy-four on January 26, 1893, at his home in Mendham, New Jersey. He is buried in Arlington National Cemetery. But, believe it or not, a fragment of skin from his thigh is on display at The Baseball Reliquary in Monrovia, California, a very unusual museum! He and his wife, Mary, had no children.

Abner Doubleday wrote three books about his life, as well as a guidebook to Gettysburg. None of them mentioned baseball, and Doubleday never claimed to have invented the game. Stephen Jay Gould, the famous scientist and baseball fan, once wrote, "Abner Doubleday didn't know a baseball from a kumquat."

But a decade or so after Doubleday died, a committee was formed to determine who invented baseball. A man from Cooperstown, New York, named

Abner Graves claimed that one day in 1839 his boyhood friend Abner Doubleday sketched out the game in the dirt with a stick. The committee liked the idea that an American hero had created "the national pastime," and the Doubleday myth was born.

As it turned out, Abner Doubleday wasn't even *in* Cooperstown in 1839. Abner Graves, the man who claimed Doubleday invented the game, eventually went insane. He murdered his wife, Minnie, and ended his life in a Colorado institution for the criminally insane.

But the Baseball Hall of Fame has exhibited a small display case with a battered old ball inside identified as the Abner Doubleday Baseball. After an explanation of the Doubleday story, the caption on the wall read, "In the hearts of those who love baseball, he is remembered as the lad in the pasture where the game was invented. Only cynics would need to know more."

Nobody really knows who invented baseball. Most likely, it evolved from other ball and bat games that had been played for hundreds of years.

The Battle of Gettysburg and the scenes of the Civil War were described in this book as accurately as possible. In three days of fighting, the North and South combined lost more than 50,000 men (plus 5,000 horses and mules).

New-York Tribune.

NEW-YORK. FRIDAY, JULY 3, 1863 PRICE THREE CENTS.

THE REBEL INVASION.

SEVERE BATTLE NEAR GETTYSBURG.

Fighting Continued Yesterday.

Heavy Attack on our First Army Corps

Brave Endurance of the Troops.

MAJOR-GEN. REYNOLDS KILLED.

TIMELY ARRIVAL OF RE-ENFORCEMENTS.

The Rebels Repulsed and Driven.

Reported Capture of 6,000 Prisoners.

The Whole Army of the Potomac Brought Up.

Strong Positions Taken During the Night.

The Army Enthusiastic and Eager for Engagement.

Special Dispatch to The N.Y. Tribune.

COLUMBIA, Pa. Thursday, July 2, 1863.

The battle opened yesterday morning, by severe skirmishing. The First and Eleventh Corps, supported by Pleasanton's cavalry and artillery, engaged with Ewell's forces, near Gettysburg, toward Bendersville. The fight continued throughout the day, with variable results.

The battle was renewed this morning, and continued up to 4 o'clock, our forces gaining upon the Rebels when our messenger left the field. Since 5 o'clock, the firing has been much heavier and more rapid, pertaining to a general engagement.

Gen. Lee's forces are said to be concentrated four miles north-east of Gettysburg. This afternoon Sedgwick's corps is reported pressing upon the rear of the enemy. The 2d Army Corps is moving up from Hanover this morning.

A newspaper report from the *New-York Tribune* on the Battle of Gettysburg

The day after the Union Army chased Robert E. Lee and his men out of Gettysburg, Ulysses S. Grant beat the Confederates at Vicksburg, Mississippi. The Civil War had reached its turning point. Lee's army was staggered, the Confederacy was divided, and the Mississippi River was opened up. Yet they would hold on for two more years before Lee surrendered.

Four months after the Battle of Gettysburg, President Lincoln went to the battlefield. He delivered his famous Gettysburg Address, dedicating a national soldiers' cemetery at the north end of Cemetery Ridge.

When the Civil War finally ended, more than 600,000 Americans had died. That is more than the combined totals of deaths in all our other wars.

A great many of those Americans were boys. Although Willie, Little John, Alexander, Rufus, and Joshua were fictional characters, as many as 420,000 men under the age of eighteen served. In fact, more than 100,000 Union soldiers were younger than fifteen years old.

Baseball during the Civil War

There is no evidence that any baseball was played during the three-day Battle of Gettysburg. I made that up. But baseball *was* played behind the lines at many Civil War battlefields. In fact, the war played a large role in spreading the new game across the country. There are even stories of games that were played between Union and Confederate soldiers.

Frederick Fairfax, a soldier in the 5th Ohio infantry, wrote this in a letter home dated April 3, 1862:

> *It is astonishing how indifferent a person can become to danger. The report of musketry is heard but a very little distance from us, yet over there on the other side of the road is most of our company playing bat ball and perhaps in less than half an hour they may be called to play a ball game of a more serious nature.*

The gory scene with Stosh and his mother in the hospital tent pretty much told it like it was. Seventy-five percent of all operations performed by Civil War doctors were amputations.

Joe Stoshack, his mother, his father, and Flip Valentini are fictional characters. Time travel does not exist.

At least not yet.

Read More!

The Civil War was one of the most important and fascinating parts of American history. If you'd like to read other stories about it, I recommend:

Banks, Sara Harrell. *Abraham's Battle: A Novel of Gettysburg*. New York: Atheneum Books, 1999.

Bartoletti, Susan Campbell. *No Man's Land: A Young Soldier's Story*. New York: Blue Sky Press, 1999.

Crisp, Marty. *Private Captain: A Story of Gettysburg*. New York: Philomel Books, 2001.

Denenberg, Barry. *When Will This Cruel War Be Over?: The Civil War Diary of Emma Simpson*. New York: Scholastic, 1996.

Ernst, Kathleen. *Retreat from Gettysburg*. Shippensburg, Pa.: White Mane Books, 2000.

Gauch, Patricia Lee. *Thunder at Gettysburg*. New York: Coward, McCann & Geoghegan, 1975.

Hunt, Irene. *Across Five Aprils*. Chicago: Follett, 1964.

Murphy, Jim. *The Journal of James Edmond Pease: A Civil War Union Soldier*. New York: Scholastic, 1998.

Osborne, Mary Pope. *My Brother's Keeper: Virginia's Diary*. New York: Scholastic, 2000.

Paulsen, Gary. *Soldier's Heart: A Novel of the Civil War*. New York: Delacorte, 1998.

Wisler, G. Clifton. *The Drummer Boy of Vicksburg*. New York: Lodestar Books, 1997.

Permissions

This author would like to acknowledge the following for use of photographs: National Baseball Hall of Fame Library, Cooperstown, NY: 30. Library of Congress: 35, 53, 57, 131, 136, 162.

More Baseball Card Adventures from

DAN GUTMAN!

Honus & Me

Jackie & Me

Babe & Me

Shoeless Joe & Me

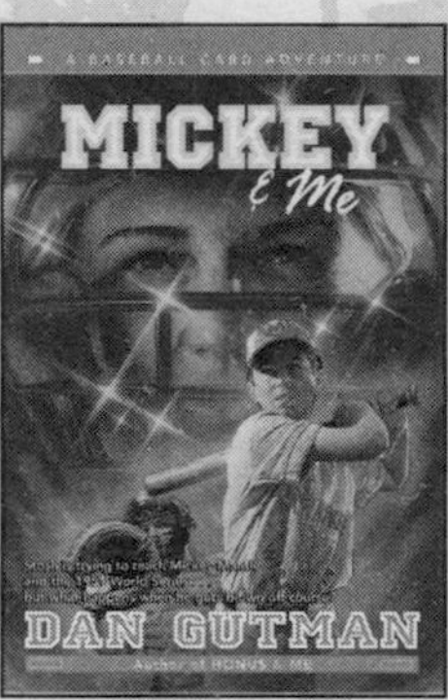

Mickey & Me

Satch & Me

Amistad

www.harpercollinschildrens.com

HarperTrophy®
An Imprint of HarperCollins*Publishers*